PRAISE FOR THE PREQUEL
IPPY GOLD MEDAL WINNER

ORDINARY SOIL

"*Ordinary Soil* brings to haunting life the desperate realities of the American heartland but also offers a glimpse into a better future . . . a call to action for all of us."

—**WOODY HARRELSON**

"An epic, beautiful, and compelling story, rich in plot and characters, with a powerful message that needs to be heard by all of us."

—**RANDY ZISK,** Producer/Director of *Monk,* Director of East New York, *The Blacklist*, *The Mentalist*, *NCIS New Orleans*, *NYPD Blue*, *The Blacklist*, *Grey's Anatomy*

"Beautifully written . . . captivates readers with an urgent call to action and a message of pure hope. Woodard eloquently weaves a tale of relatable humanity that inspires us all to embrace our connection to the earth."

—**EVAN HARRISON,** CEO of Kiss the Ground

"Captivating . . . an essential love story between earth and human."

—**JAY NAIDOO,** Cabinet Minister for Nelson Mandela

ANALOG SUN

A FABLE

ALEX WOODARD

GREENLEAF
BOOK GROUP PRESS

This book is a work of fiction. Names, characters, businesses, organizations, places, events, and incidents are either a product of the author's imagination or are used fictitiously. Any resemblance to actual persons, living or dead, events, or locales is entirely coincidental.

Published by Greenleaf Book Group Press
Austin, Texas
www.gbgpress.com

Distributed by Greenleaf Book Group

For ordering information or special discounts for bulk purchases, please contact Greenleaf Book Group at PO Box 91869, Austin, TX 78709, 512.891.6100.

Design and composition by Greenleaf Book Group
Cover design by Greenleaf Book Group
Cover Images: ikril/stock.adobe.com; aerial-drone/stock.adobe.com; Steeve/stock.adobe.com.
Filly's First Run photograph by David Stoecklein. Copyright © by David Stoecklein. Used by permission. All rights reserved.

Publisher's Cataloging-in-Publication data is available.

Print ISBN: 979-8-88645-385-0

eBook ISBN: 979-8-88645-386-7

To offset the number of trees consumed in the printing of our books, Greenleaf donates a portion of the proceeds from each printing to the Arbor Day Foundation. Greenleaf Book Group has replaced over 50,000 trees since 2007.

Printed in the United States of America on acid-free paper

25 26 27 28 29 30 31 32 10 9 8 7 6 5 4 3 2 1

First Edition

1

She blinked against the curtains of wet atmosphere hanging across the eastern front, surveying the shadows for the slightest sign of threat.

But there was no life here. The night's grinding, violent chaos had disappeared . . . gone, evaporated into body-shaped spaces left behind by the vanquished.

The thin gray stray breathed in a whisper of dank air and warily began her navigation of the abandoned battlefield, littered with sharp metal points and casings. A promising cavity opened to her left, and within a few footfalls, she found a pile of soft material that smelled of potential. She paused at the puddle of stench surrounding the scrap heap, her empty belly rumbling as she stretched across the foul pond in a careful search for an abandoned ration, maybe—

A sudden, spasmic jolt shattered her curiosity and sent her scampering for safety, her retreating eyes locked on the mass unfolding in the low fog. She held the threatening form in frame until she reached the street, lowered her head, and disappeared into the fits and starts of the waking world.

Adam forced his eyelids halfway open and studied the sideways, soot-stained brick pattern dominating his field of vision, with syringes and residue-singed scraps of foil scattered in the foreground. The heroin duvet he'd managed to drape over himself after last night's beatdown had faded to a threadbare sheet, and he put off his first conscious breath as long as he could to delay the inbound freight train of pain.

The few seconds he bought only made the reflexive gasp more violent. Agony erupted from his gut and pushed through his throat, where a scream devolved into a scrape of air against teeth, lost in the backfires and arguments already echoing from the street.

The Wild West had returned to the east side of this little beach town, where the horses were stolen shopping carts, the guns were needles, and guys like him were tumbleweeds blowing across the concrete prairie. If anybody did bother to duck their head into this alley, they'd take him for just another junkie sleeping off their high. And they'd usually be right.

But this time, the enemy without had inflicted more damage than the enemy within, and death seemed a welcome escape . . . although dying here would only validate the knowing I-told-you-so nods between the people back home who shouldn't matter and be the ultimate letdown to the people who actually did.

His gaze traveled down his prone tangle of skin and bones, from the hands that must belong to someone else to the cracked and blackened bare feet. Adam shifted his weight to his hip and lunged toward the street, his plea for forgiveness lost somewhere in the oblivion between his heart and tongue before his head even hit the asphalt.

— —

Adam's eyes flew open, fists clenched in anticipation of the excruciating pain that had welded him into the cracks of the alley. But the searing siren of torn ligaments and broken bones didn't sound, only a blunted silence riding the familiar void of feeling that he'd come to favor lately. This blissful calm, and the blinding white light now burning his corneas, could only mean that the man upstairs, whose existence up until this very moment Adam had denied, took particular mercy on the fuckups.

Swiftly converted to whatever religion might be necessary to complete this transaction, Adam tried to move toward the light, but he seemed to be straitjacketed in place. What was he supposed to do? Float there? Or—

God leaned over him, darkening heaven's gate and obstructing a clear path to salvation. Adam struggled to distinguish Her backlit features . . . All he could make out was an ample head crowned by a massive spiraled mound of hair, reminiscent of the delicious rolls he'd half-heartedly sold but whole-heartedly pilfered working at the Cinnabon outside Stillwater.

He fought the reflex to laugh at his own lame joke, not yet fully coalesced around the concept of a hairstyle called a Cinnabun. Too nervous to uncork whatever torture might be lingering, he stayed as rigid as he could.

God leaned back and lifted Her hands from his pinned forearms. "That half-ass smile might work on the other girls, but it ain't workin' on me. And don't bother trying to flirt your way to more morphine. Ain't my first rodeo."

Adam studied the shadow. "You're not God."

"No, but I do meet the eligibility requirements for a saint, because I've been basically wiping your ass since you got here."

He looked around the sparse room, which felt more like a

holding pen, without the usual tangle of wires and tubes and hospital machinery. "Where am I?"

"You got moved to a room they're still working on. Good enough for you right now, seeing as you're about ready to get out."

"How long have I—"

"Oh no you don't. I'm asking the questions. You came to me with no ID, no wallet, no next of kin—nothing. They ought to microchip your kind, like they did my cat after she fell down the fire escape. What's your deal?"

Adam raised an eyebrow and wagged an index finger. "Can't ask me that."

The nurse scoffed and shook her head. "Oh, child. Been in enough rehabs and hospitals to know the privacy rules, huh? You really want to pull the HIPAA card on somebody who just said they've pretty much been wiping your ass?"

Adam conceded the strong point with a sigh. "Fine. Trade you. Intel for intel. Help me out with how I got here."

"My understanding is that you're way back in an alley, someplace where if anybody goes, nobody cares."

"You mean *were*."

She nodded and walked toward the window. "Right. Sorry. Long shift."

"You and me both." Adam retraced the night as far back as he could. He hadn't seen anybody in the alley, except the guy who'd done this to him. But he'd also been either high or unconscious, and neither state of mind lent themselves to dependable clarity.

The nurse tugged on the stubborn blinds, trying to get them to budge. "Anyway, you're a lucky bastard with a Good Samaritan to thank. You did come to me with a few internal injuries . . . pulmonary contusion, that kind of thing, which shouldn't really bother you at this point." She glanced over her shoulder toward the open door, as if she expected someone to poke their head in. "And you still got your baby-maker."

She was right. He wasn't really hurting anywhere, but knobby knees of panic pushed through the blanket of relative calm. Where was his phone? He couldn't survive without—

"What happened, hon? Cat got your tongue? Thought you'd be happy your man parts are still intact for the next part of the ride."

"Where's my phone?"

She side-eyed him from the window and resorted to tucking the blinds under themselves to let in some early morning light. "If you had one, you don't anymore. All right, your turn . . . What happened to you?"

"You just told me what happened. Alley, bad shape, salvaged baby-maker. We're even."

The nurse turned and raised a hand over his rib cage in a mock threat to bring the hammer down on his torso, and Adam showed his palms in protest. "OK, OK. No need to pull a *Misery* on me. I honestly don't know what happened. I'd just scored and was going to smoke in the alley, and the guy who runs things around there cornered me. He said I had a debt, but he's not the type I'd stiff. Nobody messes with him. I was pretty much just in the wrong place at the wrong time."

"I see. So, you're another victim. Ain't done nothing wrong." The nurse patted him on the shin. "Poor baby." She checked her clipboard. "You can keep your story to yourself. I got a few more just like you I need to deal with."

He'd caused a lot of disappointment over the last couple of decades but still hated being that guy. "Look, I'm not saying I'm a victim. I'm just a kid from Oklahoma who stepped off the bus into more mayhem than I expected."

The nurse's pursed lips softened as she ambled around the foot of the bed. "I thought I recognized you from the 'Welcome to the Jungle' video."

"Yeah. That's me. Axl Rose, without the voice or the drive." He breathed deep, testing his lungs. Seemed OK . . . Didn't she say he'd had a pulmonary contusion? He must've been in here for a while—longer than she was letting on. "I don't know, I guess I just got a little lost."

She shot him a glance that reminded him of the oh-no-you-don't darts his mother used to throw. "Well, honey, you had at least a gram of 'lost' running through you when they handed this case over to me. That's more than a little. I'm guessing you didn't really come to California for the smack, though."

Adam shifted his eyes to the window, squinting against the glare. "No, my brother sent me on some family business, and I took a little side trip."

"Sounds like it."

"I wasn't stealing or anything. He gave me some cash for emergencies, and I stayed in cheap places."

"And by that you mean on the street."

"Mostly." He pivoted away from the potential deep dive into his moral and familial failures. "So, when am I going to get out of here?"

"Not enjoying the company? Don't tell me you're going to ding me on your Yelp review. I'm never going to climb the ladder at this rate."

"I—"

"You're ready now."

"Great. Can you get the paperwork going? I'll find a way to pay eventually—"

She shook her head. "Don't lie to me, kid. You can bypass outtake, because as far as they're concerned, you're not even here. Lost cause, covered by the powers that be. Just get yourself right, that'll be payment enough. For me, anyway." The nurse scribbled on her clipboard, tore off a corner of the paper, and put the scrap on his bedside table. "Here. A girlfriend runs this place. That's your next stop."

"OK. I—"

"Go straight there. And I'll find out if you don't show up. I don't care if I don't know you from Adam, I'll track your ass down and beat it worse than whoever did this to you."

"You do actually know me from Adam. Well, *as* Adam."

"That's your name? Damn. Wish I could still do the Powerball, if it's going to be that kind of day. All right, Adam, I gotta finish my rounds. Another one, two floors up, reminds me of you." She touched his forearm and started to move out of the room. "Go on. Get out of here. Remember, straight to rehab."

Adam realized he never did get her name, so he leaned forward and blurted out the most endearing thing that came to mind.

"All right, Mama Bear."

The ample head of tightly pulled-back hair turned ever so slightly and gave a single nod before disappearing down the hall. Adam pushed up from the bed and swung his feet to the floor. A much cleaner version of his clothes sat folded on the chair by the door, most likely courtesy of Mama Bear.

Mama Bear?

He probably should've gone with the other name he'd thought of when he first saw her silhouetted against that bright fluorescent white. Which she must have turned off when she left, because the room now only held the light cutting through the streaked window, tiny flecks of dust floating through the pillars of early morning sun lodged into the floor.

—

Adam watched the horses run, wild and free and unmoving across the stretched canvas. A young one, somewhere between foal and colt, led the small herd, his gangly, undeveloped limbs at odds with his speed.

He didn't know when the picture had been taken, but any longer than a couple of decades ago would mean that most of that herd was already gone. Maybe the young one was still alive, bucking and rearing somewhere. Probably not.

His woven fingers tightened involuntarily. Big animals left a big space when they died. When he'd watched his first dog die, he swore he saw the life actually leave the huge black Labrador and return to the air, Sooner's blood and bone shifting into something invisible. And he'd helped put his share of horses down on the farm, too, which for him meant holding the lead while his dad or Jake shot the unlucky one between the eyes. He never watched, always managing to turn his head away until he could drop the rope and leave them to dig the hole with the skid steer.

He didn't need to see the horse collapse to feel the rush of energy leaving, blowing past him into the prairie sky or some other place or person. He didn't know the destination, only that the departure was real and more noticeable even than the week he left Oklahoma, when he'd stood at his dad's bedside and watched him take his last, labored breath.

But maybe the young one in the photograph had escaped these pixelated confines into the wildness of his being, the small streak of white between his eyes now a full blaze, still bleeding into his chestnut forelock. Who knows, maybe he had more time above ground than Adam did, the way things were going.

Adam untangled his hands and pushed his palms into his knees, exhaling a breath he didn't know he'd been holding.

His focus shifted from the golden-hued prairie surrounding the young horse to the waiting room, which looked a lot like the others back home . . . a holding pen for the well-lit, well-decorated, and well-intentioned treatment centers that he'd sworn off before hitting his own rock bottom and getting clean himself.

Well, kind of clean. He hadn't intended to get shipwrecked on this particular fentanyl-laced white-sand beach. So much for the three-hour tour to see how the other, opioid-inclined half lived.

He was only in this waiting room as a thank-you to Mama Bear, which was his version of doing the right thing. But he couldn't take his eyes off that little colt. He was watching fire, lost in flames of freedom and aliveness and promise, dancing from the embers of confinement. All on a pale yellow wall with an eggshell finish.

The intake nurse had been on the phone when he showed up and had pretended like he wasn't even there as he stood in front of the plexiglass window. She was still talking, her manicured hand playing with the edges of the phone case. He stood up and got as close as he could to the photograph, staring into the young horse's eyes, then taking in every corner of the picture, including a small silver plaque engraved with the photographer's signature and the name of a mustang sanctuary in Santa Fe.

And by the time the intake nurse swiped the screen to hang up and turned her attention toward the plexiglass window, he was that little colt, running free, escaping the confines of someone else's plan into the wildness of his being on the concrete prairie.

Adam caught his breath, leaned back, and admired the day's great accomplishment, now that checking into rehab was off the table.

Pissing away the shit stains in a public restroom toilet was a far cry from what he'd been sent to California to do, which also had nothing to do with rehab. But this was hard work, rationalizing pride in the smallest of meaningless things.

Missing himself in the mirror on the way out, he eased into the river of humanity churning down the Venice boardwalk. Many of the faces were familiar now, mottled by a handful of agape tourists unversed in what this place had become.

Not that he knew what this place had been before. He'd never even seen the ocean until this field trip, so his only frame of reference was the head shop owner's wistful stories that romanticized a holdover mecca from the Summer of Love.

Apparently, the hippies had morphed into bodybuilders, then into freaks, then into a unique species of miscreant, of which he was now a card-carrying member. And overnight, the town had shifted from a relatively harmless circus to a reliable place to score whatever you needed and sleep wherever you wanted.

Adam kicked a crushed can into the sand. Overnight? Know what happened overnight? The sky got dark. Stars came out. Back home, at least. Around here, the stars were lost in the toxic haze of dirty air and light pollution, which had confused the hell out of him those first couple of nights. Anyway, that's all that really happened overnight. Everything else was a slow build that people liked to say was sudden, which let them off the hook for shit they should've handled sooner.

He slowed to a shuffle as he stared at a jet from nearby LAX inching across the sky. The contrail unfolded in slow motion, a cirrus runner along an azure hallway. He watched the plane mosey across the expanse of promise, with all the time in the world to get wherever it was going. Reaching a calloused index finger to touch the tiny tail, Adam followed his cracked fingernail down to the dirt already caked in the tiny dried creek beds of his palm. The grime felt artificial. Industrial. Not even dirt, really. Not like the ordinary soil of the family farm back in Oklahoma.

That was then, this is now.

Adam sighed and dropped his hand to his side. Nothing like using a worn cliché to bury a past still very much alive. He meandered a few feet off course, forcing a seagull from a promising McDonald's wrapper, and ignored the bird as she outpaced the streaking jet plane into yet another illusory horizon.

—

The wandering waltz between gull and toddler drifted into the periphery of the golden-hour seascape, their tiny footprints tracking an uneven helix across the wet sand. Adam squinted against the setting sun from his perch on the lifeguard stand to decipher the silica petroglyphs.

One more hit.

All right, all right, all right

He snuck another puff off the small glass-blown pipe cradled in his palm, held the smoke as long as his oxygen-starved lungs would allow, and exhaled into the battered wooden eaves above him. The haze drifted into the expanse of sky framing the overhang, where kaleidoscope cumulus clouds billowed into cirrus swirls.

A wisp of a vapor tail wagged in recognition from a vaguely canine cloud.

Hey, Sooner.

This is why he came here.

Here, where he could see the excited, rambling, black furball of energy, let loose from Santa's hiding place in the field, crashing through the corn rows on Christmas morning. Here, where he could see the big blocky head resting on his morose teenage lap as they sat on the back porch. Here, where he could see the floppy ears waving in the wind of the open window, sitting shotgun in his truck.

So many *here's*.

Even here, where he could see his own arms, already punctured by bad decisions getting worse, lowering the huge heavy body to rest under the old elm by the creek. He didn't like that *here*. But the rest?

The rest was beautiful.

A thousand little suns fought through the chemical curtain pulling across the cobalt blue, which would've been a blackout shade if he was shooting this stuff . . . but a needle would mean he'd really slipped. He let his eyelids flutter to rest, and the clouds, free of the human imposition of love, innocence, and all the beautiful things, went back to being clouds.

Which, of course, is all they ever were.

Time's up, Adam.

Adam rocketed upright into a frozen panic and peered over the edge of the platform.

The air dripped liquid with evening fog rolling in from the ocean, leaving him in a vulnerable cloud. So stupid, to have fallen asleep outside and not crawled back into his nest in the lifeguard stand. He was getting complacent, and that's when trouble tended to show up.

Like now.

He knew better than to ask out loud who was there and what they wanted. The steady rumble of the ocean answered anyway, but he hardly heard the sound of the water, let alone her response and request, against the deafening anxiety of fight-or-flight. He became as still as possible, save for the halted whispers of his quickening breath.

And if something deeper was at work, where an internal switch had finally been flipped in this natural silence to illuminate the path forward, Adam was unaware.

This lifeguard stand abandoned for winter had become a safe haven the last month, a refuge from the fight raging on the streets. But staying wasn't an option anymore, not if someone knew he was here. He battled the noise of who the voice might belong to as he ducked his head into the confines of the tower and frantically stuffed what little he had into his backpack: a couple of shirts that desperately needed to be washed in the beach parking lot shower, his sleeping bag, and a few granola bars given to him by outreach workers.

A slight rustle sounded in the corner of the cramped abode, and Adam turned in alarm to face the threat: a tiny nose quivering over the edge of the thin mattress, followed by two tiny ears and two tiny eyes. He knew what the mouse was looking for . . . They'd moved into these rotting plywood walls at around the same time, sharing Doritos and McNuggets whenever providence allowed. Adam had woken more than once to the mouse curled up in a fold of his sleeping bag, and those nights he'd dreamed himself a twenty-first-century Lennie, walking through a dystopian *Of Mice and Men* with only this tiny furball to comfort him.

Not a big black dog, but still. Didn't matter. Animals were the best kinds of people.

"OK, little guy. I gotta run. Thanks for the hang." He pulled a granola bar from his backpack, unwrapped it, and threw half the parting gift on the bed.

And for the first time since leaving Oklahoma, because he had nowhere left to go, he knew where he was going. Where he'd meant to go, where he should've gone all along: to the numbers and letters his brother had scrawled on the inside cover of a gardening book buried in his backpack.

Which he slung over his shoulder before shoving the rest of the granola bar in his mouth, hopping the rail, and hitting the soft sand at a run, never once looking back at the ocean to see where the voice may have come from.

"You must be Adam."

Adam searched his feet for any excuse but the truth. "Yeah, sorry I'm late, I—"

"Don't bother." Invisible drawers opened and closed in the darkened entry until an envelope slid under the screen door. "Here. This is for you."

Adam knelt and fingered the stiff white rectangle, his heartbeat quickening in rhythm with the woman's retreating footsteps. He turned the paper cocoon over in his hands until his thumb found the flap crease, and he watched a single yellow sheet drift onto the whitewashed planks of the porch.

He reached to rescue the letter and read as he rose.

Hello, Adam.

I wish I could say I'm pleased to meet you, but if you're reading this, I'm not saying much of anything. Out loud, anyway.

One minute you're here, next minute you're gone. I think you understand that more than you realize at the moment.

I waited as long as I could, seeing as your brother said you'd be here by Thanksgiving. I must admit, I did appreciate his reaching out, although the whispered background prompts suggested that his wife may have been the more enthusiastic party. A red-state Oklahoma farmer holding conversational hands with an occasional tree hugger from blue California? Pigs do fly, apparently. I think we truly enjoyed talking to each other, which was probably as surprising to him as it was to me.

So much so that I accepted his request to send you here. My daughter said this was clearly a telltale sign of my impending doom, especially since I'd abandoned the internship program years ago and had been refusing visitors as of late. And where would you sleep? Lions and tigers and bears, oh my.

Perhaps she was right, but at the time, I believed otherwise. Your brother's hope (and my final Hail Mary into the end zone of meaningful contribution) was that through authentic experience—getting your hands dirty—you'd learn, and more importantly feel, then bring back to him a different way of being with both the land and yourself. They are, after all, infinitely intertwined.

But hope is a cruel muse, isn't she? Fate—hope's more realistic sibling, in my view—had other plans.

And so, thanks to your tardiness and my expiration date, an attempt at truth administered through scrawled graphite is all I can give you. Why bother, you might ask? Well, you finally got here, and your brother seems like an earnest soul trying to regenerate his own life and his land, enduring considerable expense to send you west, so the least I could do is leave the two of you with a souvenir.

I'm afraid you won't find specific farming techniques here . . . just the whittling down of a lifetime into a few words that you might find useful. My time spent dying (which we're all doing, being busy living or dying . . .

Bobby Dylan sang something like that, I think, and also one of my favorites, about the unnecessary prognostication of weathermen) has left me in quite the reflective stupor. Lately I've been wondering if perhaps I should have offered fewer road maps and more compasses. I may have authored one too many detailed agricultural instruction manuals, obtuse how-to road maps written as journaled records of my own trial-and-error adventures. This is how I know that life is so much richer when we navigate our own path. Because I navigated mine.

But which compass to give you, as you embark on this most unusual journey?

I'm at a loss for words, for once. But you'll have guides along the way, if you pay attention. And I suppose if you need a directional nudge, I'd encourage you to walk in awe where the wilder things are . . . the beasts, the seasons, the beauty untouched by humans. I certainly don't believe the salve for all ills can be found by destroying humanity's cell phones and hugging a collective tree. However, I might argue (strongly, given my earlier self-declaration) that some good would come from the effort.

Until your number comes up, of course. Because

everything's going to die. But everything may be coming back, too (tip of the trowel to Springsteen).

Including you, if you play your cards right. And me.

I know this, because after burying countless dogs and horses and cows and chickens and goats and even our first son, I can tell you with authority that nothing that dies stays dead for long if they're in good dirt.

Which is where you'll find me, feeding that beautiful grand pepper tree southwest of the house. You'll see us on your way out, to your right, just before you hit the county road.

Oh, and as cruel of a muse as hope may be, she can be equally generous . . . and my sincere hope is that as you make your way, you indeed stumble toward, and perhaps find, some joy.

Good luck (unfortunately, that's still a thing).
A Hippie Farmer

Adam peered into the cavern of the farmhouse, thought better of calling goodbye to whoever was inside, and turned to face the porch stairs, still clutching the letter. He took the treads deliberately, staring at each foot not only for the short descent but also for each ensuing step along the entirety of the driveway, lost in the familiar fog of shame . . . this time for getting high instead of getting here.

So lost that he forgot to look for the pepper tree on his way out, to his right, just before he hit the county road.

2

Finally.

Adam had been trying in vain to wave down a ride for the last few hours, but every car and truck had blown by him. This ancient pickup, with onions held in the truck bed by a patchwork of splintered pallets, was the only one that had showed any sign of slowing.

The old Toyota rolled to a stop, and Adam hurried to the passenger door. As he slid onto the bench seat, his eyes caught the leathered hand holding the gear knob. His focus shifted to the shined work boots on the floorboard, then traveled up the ironed jeans to the tucked-in cowboy shirt.

"Never seen a Mexican before?"

Adam straightened in embarrassment, his lower back pushing into the vinyl seat. "No, no."

"That so? Well, today's your lucky day. You got a ride, *and* you got to see a Mexican."

Adam shut the door, bracing against the rattle of glass free from the encumbrance of weather stripping. "I meant 'no, no, that's not it.' Your clothes just seemed very neat—"

"For somebody driving a beater with root vegetables in the back?"

"Yeah. I mean, no. Sorry. Let's start over." Adam held out his hand. "I'm Adam."

"And I'm shifting into third. You can call me Max."

Adam pulled his hand back to his lap and fumbled with the strap on his backpack. "OK, Max. Where you heading?"

"Same place you're heading."

"Huh?"

"I'm going south. And now you are too."

Adam looked to his right to avoid eye contact, surprised to see the landscape already changing outside the passenger window. He'd been hitching on Highway 101 north of Salinas, but now they were leaving the verdant valley to head east into a low mountain range. "Sorry about being weird. No excuse, except that I haven't actually had a real conversation in a long, long time."

Max raised an eyebrow. "That so? This should be interesting. If we decide to converse, that is."

"I can do the talking. Good practice for reentry into society. Maybe entertaining enough to be payment for the ride."

"Ass, cash, or grass. Nobody rides for free." Max pushed in the lighter knob on the dash and pulled a hand-rolled cigarette from his chest pocket. Adam shifted his sit bones a few times in the uncomfortable silence that ensued, until the tiny hot coil ejected from the dashboard.

Max lit the cigarette, set the car lighter back in place, and rolled down the driver's-side window with the hand crank. His first exhale of smoke chased the road wind, and his second settled onto the steering wheel. "Man, I miss good tobacco. Anyway, your ass ain't my type, you look broke, and I don't smoke weed. And my cousin ripped the radio out of this thing a lifetime ago. You might as well start talking."

"So let me make sure I got this right. You were born on a farm, liked getting high more than driving a combine, took off to the city, got into trouble, ran back home with your tail between your legs, got your millionth chance to get things right, and still fucked it up."

Adam nodded and took a swig of water. "And after all that, some Good Samaritan found me passed out in an alley and got me help."

"You got that right." Max stood up from the table, took their trays, and bussed them at the trash can by the food truck. "I'm never quite sure who I'm going to pick up. You're one of the luckier bastards."

"I know. I don't deserve it. Just like I didn't deserve those tacos you just got for me. Which were incredible."

"A simple 'thank you' will do."

"Well, thank you."

"You're welcome. Best place around here. Everything else is just fast food and gas stations now."

"Where are we?"

"Santa Nella. They tried to raise horses here for stock a couple hundred years ago, but the herd kept getting set free by Natives. The original adobe was right over there."

Adam looked at the Chipotle across the interstate and tried to imagine the horses from the rehab clinic photo running wild, dodging traffic. How could a place, in such a short time window, change like—

Max interrupted his daydream with the jingling of truck keys. "Hard to believe, right? OK, let's go."

"Where?"

Max walked toward the truck and started to secure a loose pallet against the bed rail. "I'm headed to Mexico, unless the boss needs me. I try to get back there every now and then to check on family. You're with me to San Diego."

Adam glanced at the truck bed, opened the passenger door, and climbed onto the bench seat. "What about the onions?"

"What, you want one?"

"No, I'm good." A wave of exhaustion washed over Adam, a familiar final destination of his trademark meth benders back in Stillwater. He wasn't sure what to blame for this particular inability to keep his eyes open, though.

A blue service truck flew past on the interstate, its huge cylindrical back end sporting white text that read *Drain Ain't Draining? Call Jerry's Commercial Plumbing!*

He watched the truck until the lettering blurred. *Sorry, Jerry, seems like my drain is draining plenty good. Too good.*

And before Max even had opened the driver's-side door, Adam was slumped against the window, snoring lightly into the hood of his sweatshirt, unaware that what he really finally felt was safe.

"What the hell is that smell?" Adam covered his nose with the inside of his hoodie.

Max rolled up his window and closed the air vents. "Gonna be stuffy in here for a minute."

On the left side horizon of the freeway, Adam saw a slow-moving black mass that reminded him of the hot tar his dad would use to patch the barn roof. That, too, had a nasty pungency, but nowhere near as foul as this. The amorphous blob came into focus as they barreled down Interstate 5, until Adam could make out heads and tails and backs, but he couldn't tell what body part belonged to what animal.

"Are those cows?"

Max shrugged. "Not sure what you call them."

"How do you mean?"

"What kind of animals are supposed to be on top of each other like that?"

Adam's childhood neighbors had raised a lot of cattle, but he couldn't remember them reeking anything like this. The stench was overwhelming as they approached the first fence line. "Point taken."

"That place is the main meat supplier for In-N-Out Burger.

Which is why I didn't honor your hamburger request and we went to that food truck instead."

"Is the smell always this bad?"

"Everybody traveling I-5 over the last three decades, which is a lot of humanity, has enjoyed that special aroma." Max nodded toward the feedlot. "Remind you of anything?"

"Um, no. Was just thinking about that. Nothing like that on the farms back home."

"No, I meant those packed encampments in LA you were telling me about."

A defensive surge rose from Adam's gut. "Wait a minute. A lot of those people I met were decent folks who didn't have a choice. And—"

"Oh, and those cows do have a choice?" Max blinked once, slowly. "Maybe that wasn't the best example. My point is that humans shouldn't be piled on top of each other all the time. In stacked apartment buildings, crowded subways, places like that. When that happens for too long, the stench is the same. Just can't always smell it."

"I see. So, in Maxland, everyone runs free and naked through endless meadows, with flowers in their hair, eating leaves and acorns."

"Maxland. I like that. All I'm saying is when you cram

too many people together and surround them with glass and asphalt, problems pile up. Stench, like I said, of a different sort."

"Yeah, well, cities are reality."

"Coming from the kid who grew up on a farm in the middle of nowhere under starry skies. You don't know shit about cities."

Adam watched the feedlot take over the side mirror. He couldn't quite pin this Max guy down. "What's your deal, anyway? You look like a Mexican, sound like an American, and talk like Sitting Bull."

Max's eyes narrowed. Adam couldn't tell if he'd overstepped and was just about to walk back his question when Max answered. "I was born stateside to Mexican parents, so I had dual citizenship. My dad got deported when I was nine years old, my mom followed him, and I stayed in Salinas with an aunt. Which is why I sound like an American, apparently. And I used to read a lot and noticed even more. Hence the wisdom of Sitting Bull, although I wouldn't go that far. That should cover the origin stories of your nuanced assessments. As an added bonus, I'm a lot older than you think." He patted Adam's knee. "And since we're doing the label thing, you look like Jesse from *Breaking Bad*, sound like an Oklahoma peewee football coach, and talk like a third grader."

And with that bless-your-heart dismissal, Max cranked

down the window and let the rush of air take over the little truck's cockpit.

"Now, we let the wind talk."

Adam followed the moonlit Pacific out to the horizon, then ahead to the shadow silhouettes of coastal mountains diving into the water, where the land seemed to have shaken off humans once and for all.

He hadn't seen the ocean since he took off running from the lifeguard stand . . . last night? Was that just last night?

Must have been. He'd easily covered the three miles inland, down Venice Boulevard to the 405 where he'd paced the on-ramp until almost daylight for a ride. An off-duty Uber driver had finally picked him up and not balked at the address Adam had shown him in the gardening book. He'd told Adam he was headed toward Salinas and wasn't Adam a lucky bastard. A theme, by most accounts.

Adam had seen the ocean as a vast unknown, separate from the mass of humanity that pushed up against a thin playground border of sand. That was the view from his lifeguard stand, anyway. But here, the land seemed married to the sea, the hills rising to his left beginning somewhere in the deep water to his right. And he was just a traveler, skating along a temporary cut that would someday be gone. Just like him.

Max nudged his elbow. "I didn't think you could go this long without talking."

"Sorry, daydreaming."

"More like nightdreaming."

"Yeah. Where are we?"

"Camp Pendleton, northern part of San Diego County."

"Where are all the people?"

Max pointed through the windshield. "Right there. Fifteen beautiful miles away."

Adam could see lights twinkling off a point in the distance and felt a twinge of anxiety about what his options would be when Max left him. "Is that San Diego?"

"No, Oceanside. We're staying at a friend's place not far from there."

He let out a soft exhale of relief . . . He'd be OK for tonight, at least. "So, they know I'm with you."

"Sort of. Greg always assumes I'm bringing somebody with me."

Adam retraced the hours since Salinas, trying to remember if he'd seen Max with a phone. "Hang on. You couldn't call anybody even if you wanted to."

"Nope."

"Are you even real?"

"You don't have a phone, either. Are you real?"

"Somebody must have stolen it during the beatdown."

"You should thank them."

"Um, no. Can't survive these days without one."

"Is that so?"

"You say that a lot."

Max shrugged. "Well, you're awful sure of a lot of things. So, you must be right. I'm just an openhearted listener, expressing my interest in your wisdom."

"You're full of shit."

"I am."

"So how does this Greg guy know you're coming? Did you send a letter with a pigeon or something?"

"He's got an open-door policy. So do I."

"Just not a cell phone."

"Right."

"Can I ask why?"

"I'm more into living analog these days. So are you, without a cell phone and riding in this old truck that doesn't even have a digital clock."

Adam pressed his palms down his jeans, studying the smoothed denim wake. "Analog?"

"You don't know what that word means?"

"Would Jesse from *Breaking Bad* know?"

Max laughed. "Right. Low bar. Basically, analog is the opposite of digital . . . about as far away from screens as you can get and still function in society. That's what it means to me, anyway. Grounded in the physical instead of based on a computer program or an algorithm. Two cans with a string between them instead of a cell phone."

"That sounds lame."

"You want to know what's lame? Artificial intelligence. I mean, it actually has the word *artificial* in it, for fuck's sake! You might as well just be giving the very force that created you the middle finger and goddamn—"

"Easy, tiger. I didn't know wise men swore like sailors. Not that I'm one to judge."

"Sorry. I just don't get why people are celebrating AI so much. Nothing intelligent about letting ones and zeros write your first novel for you. Or be your girlfriend. It's like that movie *Her*, where the guy falls in love with a computer."

Adam traced a streak of caked dust down the passenger-side window. "Well, I doubt a recently homeless, beat-up, borderline junkie is the right person to give you an intelligent take on this. Artificial or not."

"You probably won't believe me, but I never did use the internet."

"I've had my suspicions about some of the stuff you've said, but now I know you're lying."

"I'm not."

"How is that—"

"Which is probably why I'm so sensitive to the nonhuman element. Just doesn't seem right, given my history. I was a musician before I . . . well, back in the day . . . and recorded my band's demos on an ancient bare-bones, analog tape machine in our rehearsal space. It was almost impossible to edit out mistakes. We had to live with what we made with real instruments in real time. Wasn't like these days, where people use computers to manipulate everything. Felt more authentic, more representative of reality. With the internet, and especially AI, seems like you can't trust a damn thing. Including music."

"Props for the musician thing, but—"

"You can hear what I'm talking about if you look behind the seat. I think my Walkman is back there."

"Your what?"

"A cassette player."

Adam rummaged around the cab with more indolence than enthusiasm, still not quite sure what he was looking for. "I don't see anything."

"Look under the guitar case. Actually, look in the guitar case."

Adam unlatched the clasps, pushed open the lid, and under the headstock of a beat-up Gibson saw a chunk of plastic held together by the cord tethered to ancient headphones. "That yellow thing?"

"Yeah. The tape in there is a song from my old band. A demo."

Adam lifted up the guitar, pulled the Walkman out, and let the neck drop back down. "I'm guessing you want me to listen?"

"Yeah. Especially since we're in Pendleton and all you can see is sky and sea and stars."

Adam unwound the cord, pushed back his hoodie, and put on the headphones. He hit the Play button, which surprised him by responding with a real *click*, and waited.

Voices talking, laughing. Clanking of glasses, tuning of guitars. A random snare hit. A count off: one, two, three, and—

The band launched into a homegrown, roots rock song with a simple chord progression. And then a voice.

I been laying here for hours

I can't get no sleep

Not EDM or rap, so not really his thing. But his brother loved a band with a singer who sounded just like this guy. Bison Bridge or Buffalo Town or something like that.

"THIS YOU?"

Max put his finger to his lips. "No need to yell. And yes."

"WHAT?"

Max pointed toward his ear and exaggerated his enunciation. "Listen."

Adam leaned back and closed his eyes.

Watching dreams creep off the covers

And die in the concrete

Sounded vaguely biographical, at least before the Good Samaritan got him to the hospital. Minus the heroin overdose and beatdown, of course.

All I hear is the metal grinding

Gears in the machine

All I see is the circle spinning

Round and round on the screen

It goes on and on and on and on and on

I want to find stars so bright

To outshine these neon lights

A place in time with an endless sky

That goes on and on and on and on and on

As far as Adam could tell, the song was about somebody living in a city but wanting to get out. And apparently this person was sick of screens. He hit Stop on the Walkman after the first chorus. "If this is your song, you've been thinking about this analog shit for a while."

"Yeah. You probably think a camera that captures an actual image onto real film is shit, too."

"Not probably. Definitely. My iPhone camera was dope."

"Analog is writing letters, pen to paper. Digital is texting, fingers on an autocorrecting phone screen."

"Enough with the metaphors. I get it."

A fast-incoming coastal fog started to shroud all but the brake lights in front of them, and Adam had no idea they were back in civilization until Max hit the turn signal and eased the truck off the freeway onto a small boulevard. "This pickup is all analog too, made up of physical parts, and if they break, I can fix them. I mean, it's not a horse. But nothing is slave to a computer."

"Well, I'm so happy for you, analog man. And sad for me, having to listen to this. Not the song. The song was fine. Just the sermon."

Adam could barely make out the streetlights, but Max navigated the first few turns seemingly by heart before pulling into a driveway that died into a duplex. "There's an outdoor shower around the side of the building. Use it and meet me in this unit on the left."

"But—"

"Soap is there. And beach towels. Just wrap yourself in one of those when you're done, and I'll find you some clothes. And stay quiet."

Adam crept around the corner of the duplex and stepped onto a small teak platform resting under a showerhead attached to the wall. He'd expected the water to be tap cold and swallowed a yelp when the steady stream started to steam.

He hadn't taken a hot shower since leaving Oklahoma, and he stood stone-still, with his hands at his sides, letting the water cascade over his head and down his back. And as the warmth wrapped her arms around him, he returned to a place he hadn't been since long before he left. Maybe as far back as his tweens, when he'd crawled into his mom's embrace after finding Sooner whimpering, tangled up in the barbed wire bordering the south forty.

And where now his tears were lost in a stranger's water, washing away the grime.

But not the regret.

The familiar roar of the ocean echoed through Adam's waking stupor, confusing his already jumbled sense of place. The cushions under him weren't the plywood sheets of the lifeguard stand, and the waves sounded like they were farther away. He opened his eyes to find dark green fabric splashed across his field of vision and remembered where he was.

On some guy's couch.

The clanking of ceramic and low laughter pulled his focus from the cushion to the room behind him. He turned his head just enough to see Max's back pushed against the bar separating the kitchen from the living room. Someone else had their head buried in the refrigerator, probably the same guy whose T-shirt and swim trunks Adam was wearing right now.

The couch creaked under his hip, and Max turned with a smile. "Morning, sunshine. Coffee?"

Adam surrendered to the uncomfortable introduction and rolled over onto his feet to the sound of ripping Velcro. He looked down at the trunks, now hanging by only a few threads on his bony hips, and sat back down immediately. "Sorry. Nobody needs to see that first thing in the morning."

Max laughed. "I'm the one who should be sorry, for giving you whatever I grabbed in the dark from Greg's dresser."

Adam waved sheepishly to the guy in the kitchen. "You must be Greg."

Greg came around the bar and held out his hand. He was older than Adam expected, maybe late forties, with a tan, weathered face and shock of receding blond hair that hadn't seen a brush in a long time. "And you must be Adam. Pleasure."

"You sure about that? Having a homeless guy on your couch isn't most people's idea of pleasure."

"Any friend of Max's is a friend of mine. He didn't mention the homeless thing, though."

"And who said he was my friend?" Max handed Adam a cup of coffee. "Drink up. We got some baptizing to do."

"Baptizing? Max, I'm not—"

"We're taking you to church with us."

"That's not my thing. I mean, no offense. But I didn't even know it was Sunday."

"It's not, but you're still going to church. And you're wearing this." Max threw what looked like a rubber bodysuit at Adam. "Zipper goes in the back."

"What the hell is this?"

"A wet suit. Water is in the high fifties right now."

"Water?"

"The ocean. That thing you can hear laughing through the window."

"But you said you were going—"

"To church? Yes, I did. And we are."

Twenty minutes later, Adam was lying on his belly, insulated from the sand by the thin layer of neoprene wrapped around his body. While he'd faithfully heeded the zipper-in-the-back advice, he'd also walked out of the bathroom with the too-small swim trunks and T-shirt pulled tight over the wet suit.

But he was dialed in now, a willing pawn in whatever *Gidget* beach game Max was trying to play . . . although Greg seemed to have taken charge since they got down here. He knelt next to Adam and demonstrated a weird, sudden push-up all the way to his feet. "OK, so don't be slow about it. Just push into your hands and up into a crouch, quick as you can."

Adam tried but only got as far as his knees.

"That's OK, do it again. By the tenth time, you'll get it."

"And why are we doing this?"

"Just do it again. Pop up as quick as you can."

Within a minute, Adam could push to his feet without tumbling back on his ass. He was also sucking air like he'd just run a marathon.

"OK, look to your right. Try to pop up and land sideways. Left foot forward, right foot back."

Adam couldn't even get his left foot under him before sprawling back into the sand.

"Look to your left this time. Right foot forward, left foot back."

He landed solid, like a gymnast coming off a vault, and used the triumph to catch his breath.

Greg nodded. "You're a goofy-foot."

"No need to be name-calling. We just met."

"Just means you're going to stand with your left foot back."

"Stand? On what?"

Greg pointed to Max, who was shuffling across the beach, carrying surfboards under each arm. "One of those."

Adam stood up, waving his hands in front of him. "No, no, I'm good."

"Can you swim?"

"Kind of. We used to flop around in a little spring-fed lake in the summers. But the ocean scares me. Too big. I didn't get close the whole time I was in Venice Beach."

"You'll be staying where you can touch the sand. Max, put that soft-top longboard down next to him. Adam, lie on that on your belly, like you were lying on the sand."

"Nope."

Max laid the board on the sand, and Greg put his hands on his hips. "So, you're going to let this guy drive your ass hundreds of miles and keep you alive, and then let me give you a place to stay, and when we ask a tiny thing of you, you say no?"

"Pretty much."

"Get on the board."

Adam shook his head. "No way in—"

"GET ON THE FUCKING BOARD!" The scream was guttural, from someplace deep in Greg, and Adam reflexively leaped toward Max, landing on his knees. He crawled onto the board, lay flat on his stomach, and closed his eyes. "OK, OK. Sorry. I'm on the board."

Greg's voice drifted back to a gravely calm. "Now slide yourself back a little."

Adam inched his way toward the tail.

"Push up, fast as you can, looking to the left."

He stuck the landing the first time and threw both fists in the air. "People are going to think I'm Simone Biles, if they can get past the emaciated, skinny white kid thing."

"Easy, tiger. Let's go."

Adam would have eaten sand to avoid being screamed at again, so he followed Max and Greg into the shallows, until he was in stomach-high water. Greg turned the soft-top around to face the beach and motioned to Adam. "OK, now get on the board, on your stomach, just like you did on the beach. Max is going to push you in, and I'll be next to you, telling you what to do. Which you already know. When I tell you to pop up, do it. Don't think."

Adam crawled onto the board and gripped both sides with white knuckles, his Simone Biles confidence reduced to anxiety bordering on terror. "Why are we doing this, again? I didn't sign up for drowning."

Greg patted him on the calf. "Relax. Here comes one. Small and gentle."

Max moved to the back of the board. "All right buddy, here we go." Adam braced against the forward momentum of the human push, pinching his eyelids closed until the ocean took over. And in less than a heartbeat, he was wide-eyed and weightless, propelled by something infinitely more magical than mechanical . . . and blissfully deaf to his comrades' yelling. He washed up on the sand, adrenaline coursing through his bloodstream and butterflies dancing around his belly. This was something else, this was—

"Heaven, brother!" Adam craned his neck to see Greg, waist-deep in the ocean, waving his hands in a wide halo. "Heaven!"

Max's silhouette danced against the sun. "Come back out here!"

Which he did.

Over and over and over.

He almost didn't go again that afternoon. Max and Greg stayed back, because the weatherman had called for strong winds out of the south and a potential small craft advisory, which meant the ocean was going to be a sloppy mess. Surfing was going to suck.

Which was fine, since he sucked at surfing. He'd at least been able to stand up on the board toward the end of their marathon session that morning, and he wasn't anticipating some miracle advancement in ability. But he walked down to the beach with his adopted foam board under his arm anyway, just to see if the joy he'd experienced earlier, flailing around in the ocean, had been a fluke. Fun that didn't involve pharmaceutical-grade assistance was not to be trusted.

Everybody else must have listened to the weatherman, because the beach was empty. Adam trudged across the sand warmed by the late afternoon sun, an outcast—no, a castaway—stranded here on this undiscovered stretch of coastline. He stared at the ocean, lost in the sheet glass shimmering in golden-hour glints without a trace of wind, until the soles of his feet hit wet sand.

Adam wrapped the cuff of the surfboard leash around his ankle and waded into the water until he could barely touch the bottom. And of course, the first wave coming at him was bigger than any he'd seen that morning. Remembering what he'd seen Greg do a couple of times, and despite his fearful apprehension, he pushed the board aside and dove under the white water. He held his breath in puffed-out cheeks as he opened his eyes, frantically looking for the surface to escape the chaos.

But all was quiet here, peaceful, a total vacuum of sound that he'd never experienced before. The ocean was everywhere around him, silent, touching every part of his body, holding him in suspension, weightless. Adam felt like he was being watched, as if the vastness were looking at him, considering him, supporting him, until his lungs gasped for air and he lunged toward the light.

He climbed onto the board and paddled around like Greg had shown him, sometimes submerging the foam nose by accident with his weight too far forward, sometimes getting pummeled from the side by a rogue wave, sometimes turning in time to catch the curb of white water, sometimes actually clamoring to his feet and riding to the beach.

This played on repeat, until the sun threatened to sink in the sea, and he heard Max calling from the beach. Something about dinner. Maybe leaving? He couldn't hear over the crashing waves, but he was exhausted anyway, so he pushed himself into the last wave, reveling in the absence of thought and abundance of feeling, until he coasted onto the sand.

He took off the leash, picked up the board, and trotted toward Max. The news had told him the worst, but he'd pretty much experienced the best.

Which must have been what the farmer had been getting at with that cryptic Dylan lyric in his letter. Adam had been a little confused about what he'd meant by the "unnecessary prognostication of weathermen."

He got it now.

The sun had just set, barely dinnertime on this short winter day, as they stood in line for take-out tacos and burritos at the Mexican place down the street. Adam ordered, then shoved his hands in his hoodie pockets and stepped aside, trying to find the words for an apology. "Listen, I know this is lame. I can't even buy you guys dinner tonight. I've gotten this far without cash since I got beat up, but being a mooch is getting old."

Max looked at the menu tucked under plexiglass by the cash register. "That so?"

"I guess I'm trying to say I'm sorry for being a non-contributing zero."

"That was harder for you than it needed be." Greg pulled out his wallet. "Don't worry, your time will come to pay it forward."

They waited for their food outside the tiny restaurant, Adam's hands still in his pockets, his left toe tracing a break in the pavement. "Listen, Max, I've asked a couple of times, but you keep avoiding the question. Why have you been so nice to me? Both of you. I mean, it's not like I'm a long-lost family member or some high school friend you used to know."

Adam caught Max trading a glance with Greg, who shook his head ever so slightly. "Wait, what's going on?"

Max sighed. "It's fine, Greg. He's going to find out sooner or later."

Adam pulled his hands from his pockets, now reflexively balled into fists. "Find out what?"

"Well, sometimes fate needs a little push."

"What's that supposed to mean?" Adam moved toward the safety of a chair at one of the empty plastic tables lining the sidewalk, where no one could hear what was starting to feel like either a sermon or a fight.

Max followed him. "Remember when I picked you up outside Salinas?"

"Yeah."

"I knew you were going to be there."

Adam's heart leaped into his throat as he tried to push up from the table, but Greg held his shoulders from behind. "Sit down, Adam. Don't freak out."

"Give me one reason I shouldn't be freaked out."

Max took a seat next to him. "Let's just say you have a guardian angel out there."

Adam gripped the edges of his chair, as white-knuckled as he'd been when he held the surfboard earlier that morning. "Let's just say a lot more than that."

"A mutual friend knew you needed a hand and asked me for a favor. Greg said he'd help out too."

"Bullshit. I don't have any friends left. And nobody knows where I am. Or where I've been, since I lost my phone." Adam looked around at the tables and chairs scattered around in front of the taco stand. "What the fuck, man. Are they, like, watching me right now?"

Max shook his head and sat down. "No. Look, Adam—"

"And who is this *they*?"

"A friend, just . . . a friend. Anyway, my bit part in this circus ends tonight. Greg's too. You'll be fine, though."

"Bit part? Are there other bigger parts? Jesus." Adam drove his thumbnail along a cracked groove in the table, back and forth, back and forth. "Max, you have to give me more. This is dark shit."

"Relax. A friend said you needed a ride. Greg agreed to put you up. We gave you some meals, introduced you to the ocean, and maybe gave you a couple of things to think about. That's it." Max got up from the table. "Really, it's no big deal."

"No, it's a big deal. And you're leaving now?"

"Yeah. Got another job."

"I thought you were checking on your family in Mexico. Is this all one big fucking lie?"

"Something came up. That's what Greg and I were talking about this afternoon, when you were at the beach."

"So, you're just going to drop this mystery puppeteer shit on me and bail?"

Max offered a smile and held out his hand. "I gotta run. Nothing wrong with a little outside help sometimes. Truce?"

Adam got up, pushed past Max, and stormed through the assorted early diners, who kept eating and talking and drinking, oblivious to his internal—rapidly becoming external—mayhem. He covered the two blocks to Greg's house in less than a minute, but the front door was locked, and there wasn't an open window around back. All he needed was his backpack, so he could take off for somewhere he wasn't Pinocchio to some anonymous Geppetto.

He was turning the corner from the backyard, eyes trained on his shoes, when he walked straight into the brick wall of Greg's chest. If this became a physical battle, he'd lose, so he tried to take the anger in his voice down a notch. "Can you let me in? I need my shit."

"Take a breath. Where do you think you're going to go?"

"What, are there eyes on me everywhere now?"

"I didn't mean it like that."

"Whatever. I'll figure it out. I'm not staying here."

Greg looked to the darkening evening sky and sighed. "Max, you shouldn't have said anything." He dropped his gaze back to Adam. "Listen, you have no reason to trust me. But this will eventually make sense, I promise. Stay one more night here, and I'll help you find a ride east in the morning."

"Yeah. OK. No. Max was right, this is a circus. And I'm in a really dark fucking ring right now, with these clowns steering me blindly around in circles. I'll take my chances on my own."

Greg rubbed his jaw with his palm, as if he were turning a thought over and over between his teeth. "You know what? You're right. Make your way back to your brother. Nobody's standing in your way. Not me, not anyone. And if that means leaving tonight, so be it. It's only six p.m., you could probably hitch a ride as far as Arizona and get there by ten."

"Why Arizona? And how do you know I have a brother?"

"Uh. Well." Greg stuttered and shifted his eyes to the succulents planted against the side of the house. "I guess Max must have told me."

"I didn't talk to Max about a brother. Just said I had family in Oklahoma."

"Maybe I—"

"OK, that's it. Let me into the house so I can get my shit and go."

Greg turned and headed back to the front door, which opened easily without a key, and waited outside while Adam shoved his clothes into his backpack. He blew by Greg on the way down the front stairs and was a few houses away before he bothered to turn around with a raised middle finger. But Greg was already inside, his backlit shadow against the living room window, pointing and nodding as if he were talking to someone Adam hadn't known was there.

He heard an unfamiliar clunking in his backpack and swung the unzipped bag off his shoulder to check inside. There, under his three T-shirts and the *Surfer's Journal* magazine he'd swiped from the top of Greg's toilet tank, was Max's Walkman. Left, apparently, as a reminder to live a life of splendor under an analog sun.

Whatever. He'd unload the artifact for some quick cash.

Unless finding a buyer required a time machine.

3

Adam walked warily around the campfire in an awkward game of duck, duck, goose, weaving himself between the murmurs and animated conversations springing from sporadic pockets surrounding the blaze. Every exchange seemed uninterruptable to the uninvited, and nobody had even acknowledged him.

An older man with gray plaits draped against his shoulders sat upright and unmoving, away from the fray. As Adam got closer, he noticed the deep creases lining his face, canyons he could almost crawl into.

"Mind if I sit?"

The elder offered a single nod and kept staring into the flames. Adam sat on the bare ground and tried to mimic the old man's posture by crossing his legs, but the herculean demand on his hips forced him to curl forward and wrap his forearms around his knees. He stared up at the moonless sky, lit up by more stars than he'd ever seen.

Stars so bright.

Score one for Max.

He glanced across the fire at a young couple swapping copious amounts of saliva, which seemed disrespectful to the elder next to him. Mustering his best teasing voice, he tried to break the spell. "Get a room!"

They paid him no mind. He looked to his left and tried to break the uneasy silence—uneasy to him, at least. "You're probably wondering why I'm here, huh? Got a ride in with Manny. He picked me up on 66. Know him?"

"Everyone knows everyone around here."

Another uncomfortable few breaths passed. Adam uncrossed his legs at the ankles. "Yeah, well, nobody knows me."

The old man reached behind his back for a branch and started poking the embers. "Should they? Do you have something to say?"

Adam scoffed and shook his head. "People haven't ever, and will never, be lining up to listen to somebody like me."

"People aren't the only ones who can hear you."

"What, so I'm supposed to be talking to the trees?" He toed

the dirt with his foot. "At least Manny and I got along pretty good. Said I was a kindred spirit and even offered to take me into the canyon tomorrow."

"Manny was a good boy."

"Before what? His girlfriend? That's where he said he was going when he left me here. You and I both know what they're probably doing."

The elder ignored him and moved a stray coal closer to the fire. "The canyon was made by a great flood. My people were saved by an eagle who carried them to safety and then became part of the land. You can see the eagle in the rock downriver."

"Do your people have a name?"

"*Hualapai*. People of the tall pines. We are from a band that lived on this land long before your government declared it to be our reservation. I heard the story of the eagle from my grandfather right here, where we are sitting."

The old man leaned to place the stick next to Adam, offering a glimpse past his profile, and Adam saw a single tear drop down his cheek. He did a quick inventory of the conversation. "I miss my dad. I was with him when he died, right before I came out here. So I get the tears."

"I'm not crying." He leaned closer to Adam, his face coming into clearer focus in the firelight. Adam traced the trail of the single tear into shriveled flaps of skin and felt a twinge of shock when he realized he was staring into an empty eye socket.

He tried to make his voice sound unaffected. "How did—"

"Vietnam. Agent Orange."

"Couldn't a doctor—"

"No. Too late by then."

Adam stared at the fire, not knowing what to say. "So, just one tear at a time comes out?"

"From this eye, yes." The old man rose and began his trek into the dark, his bare feet leaving a dust trail lingering in low suspension over the sacred ground. "From the other, many."

—

Adam woke at daylight to windows of pale violet opening into the canyon walls. One of these first hits of dawn filled the fissure opposite his sleeping bag, cutting up the rock face through bands of packed, hardened sediment separating eras in time. His gaze landed halfway up the canyon, on a thin demarcation between layers of strata.

Something had stood there. A dinosaur, maybe? Earth sciences had been his only passing grade senior year of high school, and even now he could hear the bearded, bespectacled substitute teacher excitedly assailing the chalkboard with rhythmic stabs, showing how each layer of sedimentary rock in the Grand Canyon used to be the desert floor. Then another however many million years piled on more land to make the next desert floor. And then another floor on top of that, and then on top of that, until Adam was lost in an ancient apartment building where different lives played out in different eras, where animals, maybe even dinosaurs, roamed and killed and died.

And now he was here, at the bottom of the earth in this natural Wonder of the World, looking up through history. Not American history. Not ancient civilization history, not world history. No kind of history that could ever be taught in a classroom, although that substitute teacher gave it a run. This was the history of a planet, rising from this sliver of riverbank, told in a language more majestic than any human could create. A language of raging storms and baking heat, of mesas and washes, of a mighty river cutting through ages in time too vast for him to even imagine.

His heartbeat quickened as a faint euphoria trickled through his fingers and began to wash over him in building waves. Barely able to manage shallow sips of air, he focused on a strata crack in the canyon wall across the river, a steadying trick he'd learned when he'd drank or taken a little too much. If he knew what this was, he could probably ride it out, but there were no drugs in his system. That he knew of, anyway.

Struggling to breathe plus a racing pulse.

Panic attack?

No. He knew anxiety and sensed no trace, even as the unfamiliar, blissful surge was growing stronger.

Which meant no need for worry.

Which meant this strange exhilaration was safe.

Which allowed the beautiful internal chaos to slow and bend as his gaze opened from the single strata crack into a vast field of vision and sounds. The towering height of the canyon wall. The first rays of sunlight filtering through the vapor rising from the river. The tumbled rush of deeper water a bass line to the melodic lapping of the river's gentler edges.

All this magic, all at once, already seen and heard but never really seen or heard, as if he now had new eyes to see, new ears to hear, but he couldn't process the inputs with his usual tools. He was in the presence of greatness, that much he knew. The rest he only felt.

He dropped his eyes to his own hands, palms down in the sand on either side of his sleeping bag, and his fingers seemed so small, but still a part of something so huge. He'd never been this far from humanity and this close to an absolute beauty so massive.

Massive, like the sky last night.

Stars so bright.

Score two for Max.

Adam finally found a breath, reached over to his backpack, and pulled out the Walkman. He needed a diversion from the beauty overload he still didn't entirely trust, and no one would see him actually using this relic . . . and Max wouldn't have the satisfaction of knowing Adam might want to hear the rest of the song.

He pushed the Play button, and the song picked up in the second verse.

I didn't come here to be glass and asphalt bound

And I don't know what they want me to see

But this is all I found

Just a million other souls together but alone

They didn't tell me the golden road would lead this far from home

It goes on and on and on and on and on

Well, he was a long way from home, but he sure wasn't glass and asphalt bound with a million other souls around. No security cameras, nobody looking over his shoulder, not even anyone in earshot to hear him yell at the top of his lungs. He hit Stop, pulled the headphones off, took as deep of a breath as lying prone in his sleeping bag would allow, and screamed. "Hellllllllooo!"

No answer. No one around, anywhere. He was just drawing his next breath when another voice took it away.

"Hellllllllooo!"

The response was faint, but it was there. Somebody had heard him.

He called again. "Who are you?"

A couple of seconds passed. "Who are you?"

He sat up in his sleeping bag and tried to sound bigger and more confident than he was. "I'm Adam!"

"I'm Adam!"

Whoa. What were the chances that the other guy's name was Adam? "No, I'm Adam!"

"No, I'm Adam!"

What the hell? How was this possible?

Adam lay back down on the sandy patch of riverbank he'd appropriated for the night. Not only was he not alone, but whoever else was down here was kind of an asshole. The voice seemed to be coming from away and above him, so he followed the layer of strata back up as far as he could. There was no way to see the top of the canyon, so his eyes dropped back down to the darkest horizontal demarcation, where an early human probably stood, right on that line, looking across the canyon at where he lay right now, and—

"You look like you've seen a ghost."

Adam bolted upright and looked to his left, where a uniformed park ranger had snuck up to squat at eye level.

"No, I—"

"Not saying you're wrong. Might've been a ghost. Parts of this canyon are almost two billion years old. Plenty of time to collect spirits."

"Sorry, I—"

The park ranger rocked back onto his sit bones. "No need to be sorry, son. But I'm sure you know you can't be down here."

"I don't know anything. I'm kind of winging it."

"Winging it all the way to the bottom of the Grand Canyon?"

"Yeah. Somebody stopped on Route 66 to give me a ride yesterday. He was going down the river last night on some moonlight adventure and let me tag along. I just went with it."

"So, before me lies the mythic love child of Jack Kerouac and Huck Finn."

"Huh?"

"Never mind. You must have come through the rez on Diamond Creek Road and put in the river there."

Adam pulled the sleeping bag up around his bare, skin-and-bones chest. "I have no idea. And I thought we were going to float along all night, but he left me here after only a couple of hours. I don't know if it was something I said or what, but—"

"Manny can be that way. He did the right thing, though. This little beach is close to a relatively easy way out of the canyon."

"Wait, you know him?"

"Everyone knows everyone around here."

"Yeah, I've heard that. How did you find me?"

"Manny called it in." He stood up, his huge frame eclipsing the sun just peeking over the canyon rim. "I have a couple of mules a hundred yards south. Come on. We gotta get a move on if we're going to get out before sundown."

Adam started to wrestle around in his sleeping bag, his

fingers fumbling for the pants and shirt he'd stuffed between his feet. "But I didn't see Manny with a phone. And there can't be any reception down—"

"Let's go." The park ranger waited for him to get dressed before grabbing him by the wrist and pulling him to his feet.

A lucky bastard, bailed out again.

They picked their way along the river rock, Adam stumbling over the unpredictable footing while the park ranger skipped lightly from each granite lily pad to the next. He half-turned to Adam as they approached the mules. "So where are you from? They didn't tell me anything about you, just that you were down at the bottom of the canyon."

"I grew up on a farm in Oklahoma."

"Live there now?"

"Not really."

"Go to college and never come back?"

"Kind of."

The park ranger stopped at the two mules and loosened the leads from the scrub oak. "I get it. I didn't graduate either."

"That's not what I meant. I didn't actually go to a class. My version of going to college was moving to Stillwater to sling weed to OSU kids."

"That's one way, I guess."

"Fed my own fun for a while, then tried other stuff, got a little too deep, and—"

The park ranger motioned toward Adam's back, reaching for his backpack and sleeping bag. "And by other stuff, you mean . . ."

"By the end I was cooking with another guy and fell in with a not great crowd. Got busted, got clean, went home, and tried to mend some fences."

"What's wrong with cooking?"

Adam laughed. "Well, we weren't cooking vegetables."

"Oh, got it. Yeah. Sorry, I was always a little naive. So why are you at the bottom of the Grand Canyon?"

"Long story."

The park ranger finished tying off Adam's backpack and sleeping bag on one of the mules and handed him a worn *Born to Wander in the Grand Canyon* hat, along with the reins. "You're going to need some sun protection other than that hoodie. And we have a long ride ahead of us. Share whatever you want, if you want."

He checked his cinch and climbed onto his mule. Adam pulled himself up into the saddle and slid his feet into the stirrups. "Wait, now I have a question."

"All right."

"Was that you, messing with me this morning?"

"Messing with you?"

"Yeah, some jackhole was yelling my own words back at me."

The park ranger nudged his mule forward. "Now you're the naive one. You haven't been in the mountains much, have you?"

"Nope, the land is flat as a third grader where I'm from. Why?"

"You've never experienced an echo in nature, then."

"No, sir, I haven't." Adam's mule plodded along on her own, almost as interested in moving quickly as being left behind.

"Nature hears you. Sometimes you get an answer back."

They left the canyon floor and began the climb up the wash lined with scraggly ponderosa pines. He turned in the saddle to look back at the layered tapestry of rock, stacked in impossible perfection. To be in awe of something no human could have ever created, this majestic canyon, and believe that something had actually heard him? And answered back?

Too much to wrap his head around right now.

Sort of smelled like hippie bullshit anyway.

They lumbered slowly up the dry riverbed. Adam stared between his mule's huge ears and within a few breaths was hypnotized by the swaying motion of the animal's back. He smiled, imagining the mule as the little colt from the rehab facility photo, streaking up the wash with reckless abandon. He'd wanted to be like that horse, wild and free, but charging out of the facility and running a few hundred feet until his wind gave out wasn't the same thing as this slow plod through sand and rock.

And maybe that's how he'd always wanted to see himself . . . wild and free . . . but now, sitting on the back of this mule, he realized that the colt in the picture was a different kind of wild and free, the kind that didn't miss curfews and appointments or have wasted lungs and track marks.

What would it be, to be *that* kind of wild and free? Where he was running, wide open, *to* something instead of *away* from something? Assuming that colt wasn't running away from a mountain lion or a semitruck, of course.

He smiled and held that photograph moment of the colt until they stopped for lunch under a rock overhang, where the park ranger pulled out sandwiches for two. Adam looked at what seemed to be a BLT and scrunched his nose. "Never been into tomatoes, really. I won't even eat anything it touches because the juice sort of infects everything. Got anything else?"

"You mean like a ride out of here?"

"Right. Sorry." Adam readied himself to hide the wince and potential gag reflex he knew was coming. He took a bite and started to chew, but this didn't taste like a tomato at all. At least the kind he remembered. Sort of delicious, actually. His face relaxed as he swallowed, and almost half the sandwich was gone before he thought to say anything else.

"Thanks."

"I'm taking you as far as Eagle Point." The park ranger eyed the horse trailer in the rearview as he eased the F-350 out of a shallow gulley a few miles from where they'd come out of the canyon. "Any idea as to your next stop? Step. I mean step."

Adam watched the bouncing reverse image of the desert in the side mirror, knowing what he wanted his next step to be but not sure how to take it. "Not really. Guess I should make my way home. I've managed to survive these last couple of days without cash or a phone, but that's just because—"

"You're a lucky bastard."

"Right. But I don't think I should be pushing that luck anymore. Bound to ricochet at some point."

"Nothing you want to do before you find a ride to Oklahoma?"

"What do you mean?"

"Nothing. Just curious. Making conversation."

They rode in silence for a few minutes, the truck skating across occasional layers of slippery sand, until Adam couldn't contain his irrational idea any longer. "OK, OK, yes, there's something I want to do. But it's far-fetched and random and ludicrous, and I don't know how—"

"Let's hear it."

"I saw a colt in a photograph a few days ago, when I was in a rehab waiting room. There was something about him. I don't know. I kept hearing the words *freedom* and *aliveness* and *promise*, just staring at the photo. I felt like he was speaking to me, know what I mean? Sounds even more ridiculous saying it out loud. But I got to wondering if he was still alive and where he might be. I saw this little plaque that said where the photo was taken, at some mustang sanctuary in Santa Fe, and sort of dreamed that I could—"

"Find him?"

"Yeah. Stupid, I know. But when I was on that mule earlier, I started thinking about the little colt again."

"Maybe that's where you're supposed to go next."

"Where I'm supposed to go next is home, with my tail between my legs. Not on a scavenger hunt for a horse that could be anywhere, including six feet under."

The setting sun was kissing the canyon rim when they pulled up to what looked like a movie set. A see-through, enclosed sidewalk jutted out from the cliff, with people gawking over the side. Adam strained to discern where the line of tourists began and ended. "What's that thing?"

"Skybridge. Looks at Eagle Point."

Adam scanned the rock faces outside the passenger window. "Where are they—"

"See where the cliff dips, there, on the other side of the canyon? Looks like—"

"An eagle. Holy shit."

"There's a Hualapai legend about—"

"I know, an old guy on the reservation told me the story last night. Man, that really does look like an eagle spreading her wings."

"Funny how a legend can feel more real when you see that kind of proof. Listen, give me a minute, OK? I gotta look into something."

The park ranger disappeared around the corner of the complex, and Adam stared at Eagle Point, imagining the raptor lifting from her granite prison and rising into freedom. He waited a few more minutes, then dug into his backpack for the Walkman. Might as well hear the rest of the song.

He put the headphones on, hit Play, and listened.

If we make the interstate tonight

We'll be far enough gone by the morning light

Maybe we could almost see stars so bright

A ripping solo followed the bridge, the melody soaring into the start of a journey somewhere. And then, an arrival.

Did you think there'd be stars so bright

You can almost see to Texas tonight

Will you stay with me for the rest of the ride

We could go on and on and on and on and on

We could go on and on and on and on and on

We could go on and on and—

A harsh rattling of glass shattered Adam's meditation. He swiveled to his right, where the park ranger was rapping on the passenger window with his knuckles. "Good news. Boss said I can get you to the interstate tonight after I drop off the mules and trailer. On my way, kind of. You're on your own after that. But it's a start."

Maybe more than a start. No need to see almost to Texas.

Just as far as Santa Fe.

4

"Excuse me, I'm looking for a horse."

"We don't sell 'em; we save 'em."

At least he was in the right place. Adam looked past the woman and traced the dirt road extending into the foothills. He'd hitched overnight from Flagstaff as far as Santa Fe but had to walk the four miles out of town on this widened wagon route cutting through the valley. The land was covered in clumps of dry grass and shrubs, with little in the way of trees or anything taller than him, which turned the sky into a massive blue dome.

Nothing motorized had passed him in the predawn hours, and this woman was the first person he'd seen since leaving Santa Fe. The weathered baseball hat pulled tight against a mountain of dark hair belied the deep creases lining her face.

He figured her to be younger than she looked, kind of like him, with the likely culprit being hard work and hard sun instead of hard drugs and hard concrete.

She was working on the other side of the wire fence, trimming hooves for the small band of horses gathered around her. Her jeans and shirt carried old, caked dust, as if she hadn't changed clothes in forever.

"No, ma'am, I don't mean to buy one. I'm just trying to find a horse I saw in a photograph that was taken here."

The wrangler looked up from where she was crouched, still holding a hoof. "Oh. It's you."

Adam put his hands up to show he meant no harm, a now instinctive reaction to years of dealing with cops and heavier players on the street. "No, no. You don't know me. Long story. I—"

"Do I look like I can listen to a long story right now?"

He rested his palm on the nose of a mare that had moved from the herd to nuzzle his wrist through the cattle gate. A foal stood at her hip, only a few months old as far as Adam could tell. "All right, real quick . . . The picture was hanging in a rehab facility. Taken by a guy named Stoecklein. David, I think. The colt gave me some hope, and—"

The woman stood up in alarm. "They didn't tell me you were a junkie. I don't usually handle—"

"I'm not a junkie. At the moment, anyway."

She bent back down and away to pick up the mare's hind hoof. "Meaning maybe you will be in a couple of minutes."

"And who is 'they'?"

"What?"

"Who's the 'they' that didn't tell you I was a junkie?"

"It's a figure of speech. Apparently, you're not the sharpest tool in the shed, either."

"Do I look like an asshole ex of yours or something?"

The woman didn't look up from picking a clod of dirt from the mare's hoof. "Now that you mention it—"

"Look, that photo of the colt meant something to me, and just because—" Adam caught his breath and used it to fight back the heat rising from his gut. "Never mind. I don't know. I thought it would be cool to actually see the horse. That's all."

She stood back up again and held out her hand. "Sorry. Being an asshole was always a defense mechanism for me. And sort of a way to test the other guy out. Some things never die, I guess. I'm Sara."

Adam, well versed in the art of masking vulnerabilities, understood and went with the pivot. "Adam."

"How long were you in rehab?"

"About three minutes. I thought you weren't interested in a long story?"

"You thought right. We got work to do." She moved to the mare's front left hoof, closest to Adam. "And what was going on in this photograph, again? Just so I know we're talking about the same horse."

"The sky had sort of a golden-hued thing happening. Whole picture, actually. The colt was small and gangly and should've been trampled by the big boys behind him, but he was running wild and free at the front of the herd."

Sara stood and looked away, wiping her nose with her wrist. "I know the one."

"The photo or the colt?"

"Both. But the colt ain't a colt anymore."

"Huh?"

"Never was, actually. That young one was a filly. Strong, fast little thing. She and I showed up here around the same time. David called that photograph *Filly's First Run*."

The small sliver of his heart that had not yet bled out through mostly self-inflicted wounds deflated, stale air from a half-dead balloon escaping into the dirt at his feet. Long shot, yeah. And silly to put that kind of meaning into a stupid photograph. But still. Animals were the best kind of people.

His silence must have unsettled her, because she turned from her crouch and studied him with softening eyes. "Oh, that mustang's not dead. All grown up, just had a little foal of her own."

"Where is she?"

"You got your hand on her right now."

The morning unfolded in a blur, a dream in hot breath and dust. The mare was smaller than he'd dared to visualize over the last few days, when he'd imagined a grand stallion running and rearing and bucking and kicking across the plains. Of course, he didn't believe he'd ever actually see the horse.

Until he did.

She seemed gentle, at least through the fence, with little to prove, more mindful of her foal than Adam. There'd always been horses on the farm when he was growing up, but they were more just tools to get a job done. And while he'd learned to hold a lead rope and sit in a saddle, he'd never really slowed down enough to notice anything special about them. Except in that photograph at the rehab place. But that was only a picture, to which he could attach any story he wanted.

Sara let the mare's hoof return gently to the ground. "She's my last one. Give me a couple of minutes. I'll introduce you to her."

Adam nodded and kept his hand on the dry softness of the mare's muzzle. Her relaxed breathing was rhythmic and hypnotic, lulling him into an open-eyed reverie. The heat from the mare's nostrils raked across the top of his palm, and he followed the tightly packed strands of short hair up to her right eye. He fell immediately into her well, where something deep, ancient, and knowing surrounded and held him.

Is this what was happening in the ocean a couple of days ago, when he felt like he was being watched? Awe and fear played tug-of-war as Adam considered the possibility. What could've been watching him? Maybe a whale, whose huge eye probably held this same kind of beauty and grace and restrained calm, hiding incredible power and—

"Vastness of spirit. That's what you're sensing." Sara's voice startled Adam out of his trance. "Hard to describe, huh?"

"How did you—"

"Takes one to know one. I could tell you were lost in her. OK, come on over."

Adam shimmied through the rails and started to put his hand on the horse's neck, but Sara touched his wrist. "Not yet. You have some understanding to do."

He took an exaggerated step backward and bowed as the foal ducked under the mare and tried to nurse. She pinned her ears back, swished her tail, and moved away from the young one.

"He's getting to be too old now. She's telling him he needs to start figuring life out on his own." Sara pointed down the fence line. "Let's hang out there for a while and give her a break."

"A break?"

"Yeah, horses avoid pressure whenever they can. They search for relief. That's why a bit works in their mouth, because they move their head toward the pressure to get away from it, and their body follows."

"I don't get it."

"Give me your arm."

Adam obliged, and Sara grabbed and pulled his forearm.

"Ow! What the f—"

Still holding his arm, she started to yank again. "Move with the pull this time."

Adam didn't have time to think of a comeback, so he took a step toward her.

"Doesn't hurt anymore, right?"

"No, except where your nails dug into my skin."

"Sorry about that. Point is, you took the pressure, and pain, away by moving toward it. Same with a horse." Sara took her hat off, long dark hair cascading down her back. "You being too close to her counts as pressure, too."

"But she was sort of nuzzling me with her nose, and seemed like she—"

"That was on her terms. When she's willing, she'll tolerate, even embrace, you." She pulled the hat back on, low over her eyes. "But not because you want it to happen."

"Which is probably why I'm still single."

Sara laughed, the first crack in her armor. "Right. I'm sure that's the only reason. OK, so there's an old cowboy saying about how the outside of a horse is good for the inside of a man."

"I think I saw that on a mug at the feed store before I left Oklahoma."

"Well, it isn't true. And not just because I'm a woman. The inside, not the outside, of the horse is what really matters. Because that's where the mirror is."

"The mirror?"

"Yeah. The horse reflects back to you whatever you are. If you're scared, the horse will be scared too. Anxious. Worried. Calm. Confident. Whatever. So the first thing you do before you approach her is to take stock of yourself. Are you scattered? Lost? Frustrated?" She leaned back against the upper fence rail. "You're going to see that in her behavior, which is a pure reaction to how she's feeling. She can't hide the truth from you. And you can't hide the truth from her. That's why the inside of her is good for the inside of you."

"So what do I do if I am lost or—"

"Change the feeling. Do whatever it takes to make you relax and recenter."

"I haven't had much luck with changing a feeling that doesn't involve ingesting something."

She smiled again, the hint of teeth and tongue sparking a small fire Adam hadn't felt in years. "Try ingesting air then."

He averted his gaze to his feet, hoping she didn't catch him staring. "I, uh—"

"For now, just close your eyes and watch your breath trickle in and out. Feel your feet on the ground, rooted in the earth. Which they are, no need to look down there to check."

Adam did as he was told, grateful to escape that small fire, which would in all likelihood leave him blistered and burned. And while the effect wasn't as immediate or strong as a hit off the pipe still in his backpack, within a few breaths he noticed a different kind of quietness in his body. "OK. Now what?"

"Let's say hello."

He opened his eyes, but the mare was gone. Sara pointed to the slow rise leading up to the main house, where Adam saw the foal dancing around the mare on the perimeter of the herd. "She's the leader and doesn't like being near the road. Never did."

"How do we call to her?"

"We don't. This isn't a My Little Pony commercial."

"A what?"

"Never mind. You're too young. Just approach her and see what happens."

Adam walked toward the herd, which didn't pay him much mind until he was about one hundred feet away. The horses raised their heads in unison and held their ground, but the mare sprinted toward the lone ponderosa in the field, her foal struggling to keep up.

He looked back at Sara, who mimed taking a deep breath and slumping her shoulders. Could the mare tell he was nervous or anxious or something? Is that why she left?

Adam wasn't sure. He felt OK—still sort of calm from whatever that meditation thing was Sara had made him do. But he closed his eyes and took a deep breath anyway, and in the stillness of his exhale, he noticed the seed of a feeling, which grew until his lungs begged for air.

Fear.

He was scared. Of what, though? He'd been around horses

his entire life, up through high school. How was this any different from—

Stilted moving pictures flashed on the film screen behind his eyes. There, a sophomore in high school, telling his rigid, Vietnam-veteran father that he didn't ask anyone to homecoming because he wasn't sure if he liked girls or not. Now, his dad pushing up from the couch and walking out before Adam can even finish the sentence, slamming the front door on his way out.

There, a nervous eighteen-year-old standing on a Stillwater street corner the summer he graduated, still unsure, waiting for a savior from the classifieds section to help him figure it out. And the guy, driving toward him, slowing down, taking a look, and abruptly speeding up.

There, a small-time dealer but big-time user, the morning after taking home a dancer from the club, waking up alone in crumpled sheets crusty with booze-infused night sweat. An engine turning over outside, she is leaving, they are always leaving, except the old Labrador, the only one to not leave by choice, to want him, to belong with him until the end.

And he is here, a lost traveler who thought he'd found another chance at that one true connection, and she, too, is leaving.

This is what he was scared of, this leaving, this not wanting him, this not belonging.

The mustang had probably felt that fear of rejection in him and run away, just like he'd been doing from anything that might run away from him.

Adam kept his eyes closed and again imagined himself rooted in the ground. Not running. Staying. One breath, two. Still some anxiety swirling around in his gut but also a sense of calm. He tried to see the fear draining into the dirt. Three breaths, four. Imagining his father wherever he was, nodding and blinking a final acceptance. Five breaths. The guy passing him on the street, slowing and rolling down the window to say he also wasn't sure, which is why he kept on driving. Six breaths. The last woman he'd been with, whispering as she left that she liked him but didn't want to hurt him—

Hot breath on the back of his hand.

She was here.

Adam ran his fingers through the mare's mane, losing his skin in the coarse strands of hair running down her neck. She leaned into his palm and nickered, catching him off guard. He let his hand drift to pause, and he slowly closed his eyes as her foal stumbled in a tight playful orbit around them.

The patter of the young horse's small hooves married the calls of an unseen crow, and Adam soon found his breath matching the mare's. When had he last touched anything living, that could acknowledge him, that could actually feel him? Since he'd buried Sooner, maybe, besides hugging his mom goodbye when he left Oklahoma to come here.

Was the suburban renegade circus he chose worth missing this? Did he savor those years of jeans hanging by a thread off bony hips, showing off the used Hilfiger underwear he got for a buck at the Goodwill in Stillwater? Or was his reward the lint in the pocket of the Raiders jacket two sizes too big, hiding a sunken chest that couldn't fight a fucking cold, let alone the junior varsity bangers he talked shit to? How about the absent Christmases and birthdays, spent dodging second chances with whomever and whatever he'd been using?

Was any of that worth missing this?

When he opened his eyes again and focused on his hand, his fingers outlined a shadow on the mustang's neck in the starlight.

Starlight?

Dark did come early this time of year, and tended to sneak up on a person, a sudden curtain drawn across the long sunsets and stubborn twilights. But still. Tonight was so awash in stars that they lit up the landscape, a thousand little suns rising and dancing across the sky, spilling a luminescence across the terrain that Adam had only seen under full moons on the farm.

Stars so bright.

Score three for Max.

He watched his fingers disappear again in the horse's mane and linger there, until his hand wasn't his anymore. The corner of his eye caught movement a few hundred feet away, up and to the right, and his gaze shifted to a second-floor window of what must have been the main house. A shadow passed across the glass and then away, the silhouette diffused by distance and linen.

"You're wanted up there."

Startled, Adam pulled his hand from the horse and turned toward Sara, who must have stealthily crept up next to him. "Me?"

"No, the horse. Yeah, you. Come on."

Adam brushed off his jeans and shirt, knowing he couldn't do anything about his appearance, and not sure why he was concerned about how he looked anyway. Probably because Sara was watching him.

They headed up the slow rise, Sara slightly in front. "How did it go?"

"Not sure I have the words yet. I haven't had that sense of . . . I don't know . . . belonging, I guess, since I buried my dog."

The silhouette of Sara's hat lifted to the night sky. "You know why?"

"Because horses and dogs aren't people."

"Well, yeah. Reminds me of this story a Native shared with

me when he passed through here. He'd heard the legend from his grandfather. They were from the Hualapai tribe, near the Grand Canyon, and—"

"Was it about an eagle in a rock? Because I met that—"

"No. Dogs and horses. He said that at the beginning, the Creator gave humans two companions for our journey through life, the Dog and the Horse, which we called 'the magic dog.' The legend goes that the two-legged, four-legged, and winged creatures all lived in harmony, until one day the mischievous Coyote started stirring shit up, telling the two-leggeds that they needed their own language, different from the animals'."

"I've known a few Coyotes."

"We all have. Anyway, the Creator heard that the Coyote was making trouble and ordered him away, but it was too late. We already had our own words that only we could understand, and we started keeping secrets from the animals. We forgot their language and started hunting them, driving them deep into the forest."

Adam kicked a small stone into the uphill brush. "Humans are the worst."

"They can be. Which is why the Creator was pissed about our betrayal and sent a giant earthquake to Earth to protect the animals. The idea was to tear this place in two. On one side would be the animals and on the other side the humans.

This scared the shit out of us, because we'd come to depend on them, but this meant that we'd be separated from them forever. So we called to the animals across the widening divide, begging them for forgiveness and pleading with them to jump back across the chasm. But the animals didn't trust us, and they retreated even farther back into the forest. They'd never truly be with us again."

"Serves the humans right. What an uplifting, heartwarming tale. Thanks."

Sara slowed as they approached the house, and Adam guessed there must be more to the story. "Yeah. I know. But that's not the end. Two animals heard us calling and came charging out of the forest to leap across the canyon, just as it was becoming too wide to cross."

"The Horse and the Dog?"

"The Horse and the Dog. The Creator told us to remember the choice that the Horse and the Dog made, and to never forget the special gift they gave to us."

"And the gift is pretty much themselves?"

"More the unconditional love embodied in their very being. That leap across the chasm."

"I actually kind of believe that one, even though I know it didn't happen like that."

They stopped at the bottom of the porch stairs, and Sara turned to face Adam. "So do I, same as I believe in the story of Jesus, even though I sure as hell am not Christian or religious or anything like that. And the story of Buddha. And the story of the Horse and the Dog. Our ancestors told these stories for a reason."

"Which is?"

"They show us the truth."

"Sounds like you've had some time to think about this." Adam made his way to the porch, took off his hat, smoothed his hair, and looked back at Sara standing at the bottom of the stairs.

She waved, winked, and smiled that smile again. "See you later, cowboy."

5

Adam heard a summoning from somewhere inside the walls, just as he was about to knock. "Come in, Adam."

The voice was muffled, but familiar. He pushed open the door and walked into the entry, anticipating polished wood banisters and fancy furniture, but the place looked abandoned. Thick pouches of cobwebs covered every corner, floorboards splintered into ragged spines. And the smell . . . dank, like the root cellar back home after a storm.

"I'm upstairs."

Adam turned toward the staircase and watched each step as he climbed, avoiding the gaps rotting through the treads. At the top of the stairs, he saw a light under a closed door at the end of the hall, but he was hesitant to go any farther. A different kind of fear was rising in him: one that had nothing to do with rejection and everything to do with torture and inquisition.

"It's all right, Adam."

He walked toward the door, turned the knob, and stepped into the room. A single lamp in the corner cast a soft light on the high-backed chair angled toward the window, where a shadow sat just out of reach of the billowing drapes.

Adam's fear metastasized into confusion. "What . . . why . . . I mean, what are you doing here?"

The figure waved Adam in. "Take a seat."

Adam walked over and eased himself into the empty chair next to him. The view from the window, even at night, wasn't what he'd expected at all. No lights shimmering from the bunkhouse or barn, no rolling plains dotted with scrub oak under the wash of starlight.

Just . . . black.

Max crossed his right leg over his left, his foot bouncing gently at the ankle. "This must seem surreal, I'm sure."

"Well, you're the last person I'd expect to see around here. You said you had another job."

"I did." They sat in silence for longer than seemed comfortable. Adam heard Max's body shifting in the chair before he cleared his throat. "So, Adam, what I'm going to tell you is a little odd."

"Because you sitting alone in the upstairs corner of some haunted house isn't odd?"

"Right. I know. Guys? Come on in."

The door creaked open, and two shadow shapes walked into the room. Adam assumed they must be ranch hands, but as they got closer, he recognized Sara and Greg. Max pointed to himself, then swept his hand across the other two. "This is . . . well . . . us. We've been your guides over the last few days."

Adam's first thought ricocheted back to Max's confession, about how he'd known where to pick Adam up and had been doing a favor for a friend by taking him to San Diego. These other two must have been in on it too. Finally, he was going to get an explanation.

"We kept you on track. There were other guides along the way . . . Manny, Mama Bear, the Hualapai elder, the park ranger—basically everyone you met, including the Uber driver. But they're helping out other folks at the moment."

Adam scanned the dim room for the red light of a camera. "I'm guessing this is some kind of fucked-up reality show."

"In a way, yeah. No cameras, though."

"What exactly is this, then? And how did you even know where to find me? And why—"

"You're going to have to trust the process here. Tall ask, I know. Bear with me."

Adam's escalating anxiety shot through the roof as he watched Greg move toward the door to block his only exit. He slouched in the chair when he heard the turning of the lock, with no choice but to surrender to what seemed to have already been decided.

"No, actually, you still have a choice. We just can't let you leave until you make it."

"So, now you're reading my mind."

"One of the perks."

"Huh?"

Max ignored him and leaned forward in the chair. "We already made ours. That's why we're here."

"What's that mean?"

"Best explanation is by way of introduction, I guess. I'll start."

For me, that day was like any other. Work, band practice, then a little something to take the edge off. Not full obliteration. Just a blunting of the day's sharper points, which kept me from being cut by reality while I slept.

We'd recorded a demo that night, on my old 4-track Tascam set up in the corner of our rehearsal space. I mixed it down to a cassette tape after the band left and listened to the song on my Walkman on the way home. A few musicians had just started playing around with digital recording, but the gear was so expensive and cumbersome. I couldn't afford nice clothes, let alone recording gear. Didn't matter, though. I loved the warmth of the analog tape sound and knew how to get all I needed out of that Tascam.

And this song was good. My hands were shoved in my coat pockets, where I held the Walkman and kept rewinding as I walked, searching for where the lyrics or music needed work. But this one seemed solid. And the band sounded great. Better than ever. I felt like we were right there, you know? We just needed that break. That's a cliché, but it's also the truth. Sometimes clichés are what they are for a reason.

And that break was getting harder to come by. In the few years since I'd moved to Seattle, the major labels had closed their satellite doors, and some of the better clubs were being converted into mixed-use loft spaces for the exact opposite kind of people who had made the city the grunge capital of the world. I mean, a struggling-to-make-it Kurt Cobain was not going to be buying underwear at a Tommy Hilfiger store on his way upstairs to his two-bedroom penthouse with a view of the Space Needle.

So I was a little late to the party. I guess it took a couple of years to cut the umbilical cord of my parents' expectations and convince myself that leaving that little ag town on the Central Coast was a good idea. My folks wanted a better, more stable life for me, which is why they left me with my aunt in California when my dad got deported. They didn't really see quitting my decent farm job to be a flailing rock star as a better, more stable life, and were pretty pissed the night I told them my intent on our weekly Sunday collect call.

That's the thing, though. I didn't really want to be a rock star. I just wanted to keep writing songs and play them for an audience and record them in a studio, preferably using something other than that Tascam 4-track I'd set up on my bed. Every minute I wasn't working, sleeping, or helping my aunt with chores, I was in my room with my guitar.

And if my fingers hurt from playing, I was holding a book. I'd been like that since I was a kid, reading through my aunt's entire library of Thoreau and Dostoevsky and Steinbeck. I loved getting lost in story and language and other worlds. The music thing started to take over when my dad got deported. He'd shown me a few chords and left me his acoustic guitar, and I played that thing all the time as a way to be close to him. His fingers had made these grooves in the fretboard, and when I put my own fingers there, I felt like I was touching him. Holding his hand, almost.

Anyway, I started messing around with my own lyrics and music in high school as a way to process all the bullshit that goes on there. I thought I'd found my calling, I guess, in filtering all the stories I'd read through my own experience and into songs. And I wanted to play them for people who actually wanted to listen, although I didn't know how to even start going about that.

But I packed up the truck anyway, and headed north to the Emerald City, where all these incredible bands were born. I wasn't looking to be in a grunge band, but Seattle seemed to be where the scene was happening, so I went. Simple as that. And the place wasn't totally dead yet, not like it is now . . . like –

I was just a little late, like I said.

I had a cousin in Seattle, who said he'd let me crash on his couch until I got my feet on the ground. One night we walked the few blocks to this hole-in-the-wall joint, where some guy who looked like an Elvis impersonator was behind the bar, hosting something called an "open mic."

Turns out you could sign up every Wednesday to play a couple songs on the tiny stage in the corner. The place held a smattering of men dressed like Chris Cornell and Eddie Vedder, and one woman who looked like she was ready to go onstage at Lilith Fair, all with guitars at their feet.

My cousin knew why I'd come to Seattle and talked me into signing up the next Wednesday. I did, and I sucked, but I had at least taken a step. Which was huge, because, like I said, I had no idea how or where to start. I'd never been on a stage, or in front of a microphone, before that first open mic night.

Fast forward past a lot of dues being paid—newspaper classifieds looking for band members, finding a rehearsal space, first gig at a sports bar, shows played to absolutely no one besides the bartender—to that night we recorded the demo.

I was walking, I remember, hands in pockets, listening. That night was like most in Seattle. Couldn't see the stars. And it wasn't raining, which didn't really bother me anyway . . . The more suffocating problem was the almost constant low ceiling of cloud cover, which pushed the city lights back down until the sky was just a dull haze. That's where that song on the Walkman came from . . . "Stars So Bright."

I mouthed along to my own words pushing through the headphones as I walked through Pioneer Square. I could almost feel the city in my eyes, small wet reflections of the Central Saloon neon window light, the cigarette ground into a concrete crack, the slime of the gutter apron that hadn't seen the sun in too long.

I didn't come here to be glass and asphalt bound

And I don't know what they want me to see

But this is all I found

Just a million other souls

Together but alone

They didn't tell me the golden road

Would lead me this far from home

I want to find stars so bright to outshine these neon lights

A place in time with an endless sky that goes on and on

Nights like these, I just wanted to get out, you know? Everything about the city had started to grind me down, until I was scared about becoming just another cigarette in the concrete crack. Downtown was so damn dirty back then, at least where we were living. A petri dish, where grunge grew into . . .

well, grunge. Good for starting a musical revolution, maybe. Not so much for living.

I passed by the shell of a building I'd spent the last few days standing in front of. No, not panhandling. I was working for a traffic control company so I could keep my nights free. There was so much construction going on back then, with those clubs I told you about getting converted into bougie bullshit. I'd stood there most of the week holding an orange sign so cars and trucks could pass me by while authentic worlds got torn down behind me.

I wanted to get out, but I also didn't want to give up. I really felt like we were almost there, and to quit now would be throwing away a dream that was about to come true. So I'd just "get out" on a short-term basis that night, maybe smoke a little with my bass player and have him listen to this song on the Walkman. He felt the same way I did about how close we were to making it, and I knew he'd love how this song sounded. Even if it was recorded on a shitty Tascam.

I took a left on Yesler and headed toward the apartment we shared. Yesler was the original urban Skid Row in the 1850s, which they called Skid Road back in the day because they used to skid logs down the wet dirt road to the harbor, and people who'd fallen on hard times would go there looking for work.

And while the neighborhood when I lived there wasn't great, it also wasn't that bad anymore, and I wasn't looking for work . . . I was just looking to get home and hang out with a friend, who should've been home from rehearsal for a while now, since I'd stayed after practice to mix that song down.

I walked into our apartment, and there had to be ten or twelve people crammed into the tiny living room. Sometimes that happened in our ever-expanding circle of barely friends. Parties would just kind of erupt, even when you weren't home, especially if somebody had scored something good.

I looked around for my bass player to see if he wanted to listen to the song out on the fire escape and maybe have a smoke. And I know I've already said it, but I only ever just did enough to take the edge off. Kind of made me feel like I was in a cocoon, but in open space, without having to go anywhere. I wasn't touching the face of God or anything, but the glass and asphalt and grime and concrete would sort of melt away, and I'd almost always be transported to a field of wildflowers overlooking the ocean.

Home.

When there's a bloom, there can be wildflowers on the coast from Point Conception all the way up to Salinas, right where I picked you up. Like nothing you've ever seen, until you've seen it.

I guess sometimes I just wanted to be in bloom again.

You have to remember—actually, why would you know this, you're too young—there was a *New York Times* article back then listing Seattle's three principal drugs as "espresso, beer, and heroin." And that was true. When you're in the culture, everything is normalized, and you don't think twice about smoking a little here and there. At least I didn't. Probably sounds insane to you, with all the fentanyl-laced horror stories these days, but at parties like the one in our apartment, it wasn't seen as all that different from weed.

I'm not talking about shooting it . . . That was still pretty much confined to club bathroom stalls and locked bedrooms. We all knew musicians who had died of overdoses, going back to the Mother Love Bone guy five or six years before, in 1990. So we stayed away from the needles. Most of us, anyway. Most of the time.

So why did I try it for the first time that night? I don't know. I could come up with a lot of reasons, I guess, including being in the wrong room with the wrong people. But you know what? Nobody made me do it. Nobody pinned me down on the floor and shoved a needle in my arm. I just was curious.

Which makes what happened sort of . . .

"Tragic?" Greg emerged from the shadows to Max's left and touched his shoulder.

"Or stupid?" Max stood up and offered the chair to Greg, who shook his head.

"You're not stupid. There's a reason you've been the leader around here for a while, longer than any of us." He flopped down next to Adam and leaned forward, forearms on his thighs, hands clasped. "OK, Adam. First things first. I didn't plan on being in the hospital that night."

No, in fact, that day was supposed to end very differently.

The first winter swell had finally hit, which turned out to be *The* swell, capital *T*, the reason the beach peacocks are probably still puffing out their feathers in their where-were-you-when struts. Because, of course, triple-overhead surf should be memorialized with the same sort of reverence as the day the Twin Towers got hit.

Humans.

Anyway, I was in the parking lot, watching the first pulses pound the lineup from the safety of my truck cab. Some guy with an ample gut spilling over jeans stretched to the breaking point was doing laps in between cars, repeating over and over how his buddy spent so much money on cocaine, booze, and cigarettes that he should be able to afford better equipment for days like today.

This particular buddy, unlike his tattletale friend who didn't seem willing to leave the protection of the parking lot, was at least out there in the water. But he was struggling to paddle out on a longboard, and I found perverse redemption in watching him get hammered. Because maybe I didn't know the guy, but I knew the type. Cocaine, booze, and cigarettes has a particular smell, one which I'd either always been too afraid or not cool enough to fully embrace.

My growing allergy to people didn't help, either. I'd never really hated anyone, but at some point around forty, I finally gave myself permission to stop giving a shit what other people thought. Most folks my age were still going strong with trying to fuck the Joneses and post the love child on Instagram. Which I helped create. More on that later. Surprised I'm not in hell already.

But I'm not most folks. Funny thing is, neither is anyone, if they're honest with themselves.

I actually worried that I harbored some sort of sociopathic bend when I was in my late twenties, since I couldn't get worked up about the same stuff other people did. Most people I knew were already married and having kids, and I guess I didn't react with enough wistful admiration to their descriptions of the glorious vistas on their family-building journey. They didn't talk much about the gaping abysses they went through, which I knew must be there. Just big fucking beauty everywhere they looked, which I was told I'd only understand when I had kids of my own. Might as well have just patted me on the knee.

I wasn't against it. Having kids, that is. Just didn't happen. Kind of wish it had, but I was waiting on a willing partner, and that didn't happen either. My twenties were about women not thinking I was good enough, my thirties were about me not thinking they were good enough, and my early forties were about watching friends go through their second divorces and thinking maybe no one is good enough for anyone.

Back to that day of the big swell. I was still dry when I left the preacher in the parking lot, and the wiser move would've been to stay that way. That's looking back, of course. In the moment, I was just doing my thing.

Which I'd been lucky enough to do for a long time. I'd lived on my own terms, for better or worse, for almost thirty years.

Sure, "own terms" had a caveat or two . . . lingering parental expectations, pressures to fit in, and so on. You know the drill. But my decisions had pretty much been my own, and lately I'd started to accept the outcomes and reverberations. Like I said, for better or worse.

So the fact that I decided to paddle out that day, especially after not surfing for a couple of years, was just that—my call. And my judgment was completely shot, like everything else, given that I hadn't been doing the one thing I'd come to depend on for both mental and physical well-being. Sounds woo-woo, I know. But sometimes woo-woo shit is in the ballpark, just like Max said clichés are. Speaking of, I saw one on a T-shirt back in the day that said "tears, sweat, and the sea can cure almost anything." Case in point.

Considering my total lack of preparedness that morning, I needed an oceanic room that wasn't hosting amateur hour. Waves that big aren't only a massive physical challenge to navigate, they're also a magnet for variations on the cocaine-booze-cigarettes guy who want to brag about how they totally went out during that huge surf and laughed at Mother Nature's fury. And whose ditched boards morph into spears shooting blindly at unlucky neoprene prey. Best to choose wisely as far as arena goes, on that kind of day.

And that meant somewhere familiar. My usual break seemed to be shutting down, with the size of the swell overwhelming the reef. Still, from where I stood on the seawall, I could see a few tiny floating ants. Even though I'd been gone a while, I probably knew those guys, which would at least make for some conversation when we weren't getting pounded.

So I suited up and paddled out, hands dancing with hypothermia within the first few strokes. I ducked under the first big wave and tried to ignore the ice-cream headache dished out by the cold, churning white water. The water temp was smack in the middle of Dr. Google's recommended ice bath range, which I'd looked up when I was wondering if I'd been already engaging in this trendy wellness behavior for almost four decades.

Turns out, I had. Wait, that's not true. I told you there were a couple of years when I wasn't surfing at all. If I had been, things may have different. I'll get to that.

Anyway, I took a few more waves on the head before drifting into the lineup, already tired from being so out of shape. I was right: I knew everybody out there, all three of them. Older than me, but not by much, which made me feel better about my survival chances . . . although I'd probably never leave the house if I knew what my chances really were, with anything.

I waited awhile, watching how and where and when the ocean moved. The bigger waves were closing out, but the relatively less-towering ones offered a corner that connected all the way through to the beach. A head-high set showed on the horizon, and I turned to paddle for the third wave, guessing there'd be a lull afterward. I didn't need to get crushed on the inside by one of those bigger monsters.

The wave was a beautiful curving wall, opening up in front of me like a kaleidoscope shifting from turquoise to deep cobalt to sea green. I trailed my fingers through the face and stood as still as I could, letting the hydric power push me faster and faster, held in place by the three fins channeling water under my feet. And there was nothing else, only the thunder of white water as a soundtrack to the joy and adrenaline and peace that blooms in the absence of manufactured noise.

I pulled out before the wave shut down and decided to be done, like I was with a lot of other things at that point. Small things, really. Playing video games with random strangers online at two a.m. Wolfing down Jack in the Box dinners on the way home from my new job at the Apple Store. Stuff like that.

I'd just started working there, helping people buy more shit to take them away from what matters. Nothing against the crew on the floor with me . . . We were all just trying to make rent or tuition or child support or whatever. And it might not seem like that job fits me, but even as a kid, I loved everything tech. I was hyper detail oriented, type A, super on top of it. They'd probably diagnose me with a spin on ADHD these days, like every other kid who can't sit still and doesn't have a healthy fear of discipline from their parents.

So, yeah . . . the Apple Store. Before that, I'd actually been a software developer. Java, Python, C#, HTML, CSS, JavaScript, PHP—if I didn't know the language, I'd learn it. I loved everything about programming and coding. Shit lined up. Made sense.

And because I loved it, I was good at it. Didn't even have to go to college to get a gig in-house with a San Diego video game studio, surfing in the mornings before work and living in a duplex a few blocks from the beach. Even though I had to be in front of a screen most of the day, the company owners were militant about the work-life thing, giving us Fridays off and not caring about hours, as long as we stayed on deadline. That's why I was there for a long time until I got recruited by a small tech company in Silicon Valley with big promises of stock options and a baller lifestyle. They told me that if I hung in there, there'd come a time when I wouldn't have to work at all. As in, ever again.

I'm still not sure why I fell for it. Just before I took the job, I'd convinced myself that I'd give up my life outside of work for a few years . . . only until they went public and I could cash in my options to spend the rest of my life surfing all over the world. I was going to be chartering boats in the Mentawais, staying in oceanfront villas in the Maldives, buying a spread in Hawaii. Which, ironically, led to the no-surfing era I told you about earlier, because I moved up to Silicon Valley to be one of the lead developers for what would become Instagram. Can you believe that? Instagram!

This was before the company was bought by Facebook, or Meta, or whatever they're calling it now. The atmosphere was electric back then, everywhere you went in the Bay Area, but especially the city. By the city, I mean the San Francisco that existed before people started shooting up in the Macy's foyer and taking dumps on street corners. Me and my team tore that place up, in the way that no one thinks is cool except the douchebags doing the tearing up.

I mean, really. We were idiots as far as reading the room goes. And I was old by their standards, early thirties, but I tried to go just as hard as they did and got just as little interest from the women who pretty much turned and ran when they saw us coming.

For a while, anyway. Because who needs to meet a girl at a bar, much less have a girlfriend, when you have PornHub? The internet had grown some serious teeth by then, and I could get whatever I wanted, right there on my phone—everything from food to underwear to sex without even leaving the house. Like everybody else I knew, I was living more and more on the internet, trying to make sense of a world that wasn't ever going to make sense. No world that only exists in some artificial clusterfuck of ones and zeros and semiconductors and pixels is ever going to make sense.

Don't have to be a rocket scientist to follow this thread, right? Shit started going sideways. I went out less, because I didn't have to, and got more into gaming as a way to let off steam. As if I'd have had time anyway, since we're talking about the days when huge venture capital money started pouring into social media companies like ours. Those gourmet cafeteria and coffee bar perks only existed because most of us were sleeping under our desks and weren't exactly encouraged to leave.

But when I did go home, I'd sometimes play until three, four in the morning, sleep for a couple of hours, then maybe do a bump so I could get to work by seven thirty. Probably not a shock that I started to slip in progressively consequential ways at work and got fired before I even vested in any options.

A friend of mine back home was managing the Apple Store in Carlsbad and offered me a couch and a job. I'd only been there a week when that swell showed up, and gravity hit me hard after that one beautiful wave . . . the gravity of nothing, because that's what everything was adding up to. I guess sometimes the empty just piles on until it gets too heavy to carry.

Who knew nothing could weigh so much.

Which is why I let that weight pull me down, below the surface, into the deep. I wanted that joy and adrenaline and peace that blooms in the absence of manufactured noise to replace the emptiness forever.

As I sank, I reached down to pull off my leash, so I wouldn't be attached to the board floating above me. Apparently, I wasn't quick enough, because just as I started to black out, a hand clasped over mine. Somebody had seen the board without a rider, paddled over, and followed the leash down to me.

Next thing I knew, I was in the hospital on a vent. Wasn't part of the plan, like I said. And instead of carrying that last wave with me into the forever after, I listened to voices coming in and out of range telling me, without telling me, that I wasn't going to make it. They thought I couldn't hear them, but they thought wrong, and let me tell you, the news was not good.

But being in a coma for a while did give me a little time to ask myself some questions. Like, why did I end up spending more time in a dark room, playing Halo 3 with kids half my age, than in the ocean?

I mean, I knew the "how" . . . I just gave you the short-attention-span version . . . but not the—

"Why? That's the million-dollar question, isn't it?" Sara's fingers trailed the edge of Adam's chair as she walked around him. "Why do we make these choices?"

Greg pushed himself up and bowed to Sara. "Who knows. Not me. All I know is I could've made a different one. It's not like I didn't know better." He waved his hand in a flourish toward the open seat. "My lady, your throne."

She smiled and eased herself into the chair. "I think you know I'd rather be sitting on one of those—"

Horses. Always been my thing, far back as I can remember. I never gave a shit about dolls or stuffed animals or anything fake. Only one thing was scribbled on my first Christmas list: REEL

PONI. All caps, on one of those subscription postcards that falls out of magazines.

Apparently, a REEL PONI didn't fit down the chimney. Or, in our case, the flue for the woodstove that my dad had ill-advisedly installed in our trailer after refusing to pay for propane. I told my mom that if that fat-ass old man in his bulky suit could squeeze through a skinny metal tube to leave me a bullshit cracked plastic horse from the Dollar Store, he sure as hell could've figured out how to make a real pony fit. I was six, I think. Had a mouth on me, even back then, which I probably got from my rodeo dad. That's about all I got from him. Bastard.

I'm not sure where or when my love affair with horses began. Our neighbor had a few mixed in with other livestock, and one of my earliest memories is of my mom pulling me back through their barbed wire fence, which I'd crawled under so I could get closer to the herd. One of the barbs left a scar like a lightning bolt on my back. Must've hurt like hell, but I didn't care enough to remember.

By the time I was nine, I was here, at this ranch, mucking stalls in the barn for the occasional chance at a riding lesson. We lived in the sticks, about twenty miles away, and this shithole boarding facility was the only place around that didn't have snooty chicks from Santa Fe walking around in britches that cost more than our rent every month.

This place wasn't a shithole for long, though, if I do say so myself. I spent the summer before middle school doing whatever a twelve-year-old could do to turn it around, and sometimes I did get paid in riding lessons, but usually I got nothing. You know why I did it anyway? Because those horses had to live here. Those beautiful, willing, huge beasts didn't choose to be in this place, eating shitty hay off the manure-smeared ground in twelve-by-sixteen stalls with rusty nails begging to snag skin. The barn owner called it "deferred maintenance," but that's just another way of saying "depending on humans to do the right thing," which I was starting to believe was not a viable assumption.

So after mucking stalls, I'd pull those rusty nails. Hose down stall mats. Pick through moldy hay for the decent stuff. Sometimes, if no one was there, I'd take as many horses as I could out and walk them around on a lead. That kind of thing, all summer. My mom would drop me off on her way to work at the supermarket and pick me up after her shift, and I'd be counting down the hours until I could go back.

Couldn't say the same thing about school, once that started up in September. The learning part was OK, but the other shit was not. Most of the middle school girls had this weird, mean, dramatic vibe, which was totally foreign to me. Before I even stepped off the rural bus that first day, they'd already split themselves into cliques based on how much money their parents had and whose house had a pool.

We had one, of the vinyl kiddie variety, stashed under the deck attached to our trailer. That didn't count, which I found out when I let it slip that yeah, we totally had a pool that my mom had brought home from the housewares aisle at her supermarket job. I was promptly dismissed to my own table in the corner of the lunchroom, where I remained for the rest of middle school after one of the popular girls told me to stay away because I smelled like a barn. Which I probably did, seeing as my clothes hadn't hit the laundromat yet that week, and I was still working here on weekends.

Folks who boarded their horses would visit every once in a while. One guy, the sheriff, would drop by on Saturdays in his $60,000 truck that never saw a lick of dirt, and he'd sometimes ride one of his horses through the foothills. But he didn't do shit as far as actually caring for them. Nobody did.

Except me, starting the summer before ninth grade. If I didn't know how to do something, I'd ask my dad, and once in a beautiful blue moon, when he was still around and not hammered, he'd take me to the tack store, help me buy supplements and grooming supplies, and show me what to do.

Bathing, feeding, exercising . . . I did everything for those horses that their owners wouldn't do. Hell, I even learned how to trim their hooves. Couldn't shoe them, because that took more strength and money and steel than I had, but I kept their feet healthy. Which goes a long way in keeping the whole horse healthy. Learned that from my dad, too. I got a couple of things from him, I guess.

Anyway, I can remember probably ten or twelve horses around at any given time, but one in particular had been there ever since I started mucking stalls. She was a mustang, abandoned as a foal by some lady who ripped the little thing away from her mom because she'd seen enough social media posts to convince her that raising a baby horse would be super cute. Until she stopped showing up at the barn, for the same reason all the animal shelters fill up after Christmas: Reality is a lot different from an Instagram reel.

That mustang and I grew up together, I guess. My dad was almost out of the picture when he started her under saddle, as a favor to the barn owner. I think he owed him money . . . He owed everybody money. But at least he put me on her. She was about four, and I was in my second year of middle school at the time, which is also about when I started crying into her shoulder on the weekends. Riding and crying, that was us, all the way until my sophomore year of high school. She'd wait for me at the stall door, nicker, bury her muzzle in the crook of my arm—all that stuff you hear about in sappy girl-loves-horse stories.

Except it was real.

Sophomore year I got promoted, if you can call it that, to barn manager, which turned what I'd done for fun into a J-O-B after school and on weekends. I made a little money, and sometimes a wealthier client would throw me a holiday bone. But I wasn't sure the collateral bullshit of dealing with humans was worth it, so I didn't know what I was going to do after high school. Assuming I survived without killing somebody.

Because high school was turning out to be a bigger version of junior high's mean girl club, kind of like an amplified *Pretty in Pink* without the redemption. I'll spare you those details, because they don't deserve any more power than I've already given them. Suffice to say that my defensive shield had evolved to a near Shakespearean level of cussing while pretending not to care, but it didn't do much to keep the passive-aggressive, and sometimes just aggressive, bullshit from tearing me apart. Not that there's anything wrong with somebody lining your locker with smears of horse shit as a reminder of what you smell like. Happens to everyone, right?

I wish I could say it didn't bother me, but it did. I let myself get stuck in this black-hole spiral of giving a shit about being liked by people who didn't matter, and while I wasn't really going to kill anybody, I was starting to die a slow metaphorical death myself. Which probably would have happened for real if I got held back another year, so I buckled down as a senior and fought through the darkness to graduate. I'm convinced now that the only real joy I'd ever had, which was given to me by that mustang, had been slowly stolen by all those people who didn't matter. I just wasn't paying enough attention to notice.

Because by the time I met Daryll, the week after graduation, this barn was just a place I worked. I don't like to talk about it, even now. Too painful, too much regret. All I'll say is that mustang still came to the stall door, still nickered, still tried to bury her muzzle in the crook of my arm. But I didn't see her anymore. I just walked right past her on my way to check my makeup in the tack room mirror.

That's why I'm here now. I'm never going to let her down again. Her foal either.

Which brings me to my other love affair, the one not with the mustang. I know right where and when that one started. And right where and when it ended, too.

Started the weekend after graduation, when the sheriff brought his nephew to the barn. Good looking, his own ride, all his teeth. He'd just moved to Santa Fe from Albuquerque, and when he asked me out, I felt like I'd won the lottery. I found out later that Daryll had gotten into trouble at home, and his parents had sent him to his law-enforcing uncle to get his shit together. But he gave me the time of day.

You know that song "Fast Car"? That was me. Us, I guess. Me and Daryll. I mean, maybe not the whole song. My own dad was long gone by then, so I wasn't taking care of my old man like the girl in the song does. But Daryll did have a fast car, and he did wrap his arm around me as we raced through the city, and I did feel like I belonged.

I still went to work and did what I was supposed to do, but all I really cared about was Daryll pulling up in that fast car and us spending the night racing around from convenience store to drive-in to wherever else the night road might go. July and August flew by in a blur of headlights and back seat shenanigans, and by September, I'd quit the barn to start working at the supermarket.

My mom got me the job because I'd had a surprise positive test in the bathroom of the same store and needed the benefits package.

Daryll never hit me. But that autumn, he changed. Maybe he was pissed about me not wanting to give up the baby. I don't know. He started criticizing how I looked, what I was wearing. Sometimes even how I smelled, like those girls did in high school, even though I was working mad hours as a checkout girl and hadn't been around any horses in a long time.

By October, I'd put on a little weight because I was starting to show. He didn't like that, either. But he said he was willing to put up with my fat ass and this unborn kid as long as I brought home a paycheck and "did my part." Which pretty much meant jacking him off in that fast car after my shift. Talk about Shakespearean. He had a gift.

The supermarket was packed that Wednesday night with people buying last-minute groceries for Thanksgiving, so I was late coming out of the store. I knew he'd be mad at having to wait. He was already a few pulls deep into a fifth of Fireball by the time I collapsed into the passenger seat. Told me that my daddy had left me for a reason, so I'd better do what I could to hold on to the only man who would tolerate me. And making him wait was not on that list.

And you know what? I took it. I even said something about how he was right, and I'd be better. I'd hold on tight. Daryll handed me the Fireball and nodded for me to take a drink. I meant to fake a swallow, but he was watching, so I forced a gulp down and handed the bottle back to him. He drained the rest, threw the empty out of the driver's-side window, and peeled out of the supermarket parking lot. And within a couple of blocks, we were racing around like the good old days, which was all of six months before, trying to get back to where we'd started. Flying, on both Fireball and the 375 horses under the hood.

Except there were no horses under that hood. What a crock-of-shit expression. Nobody can shove the spirit and power of 375 horses under a thin slab of metal . . . only pistons and grease and wires and whatever other human-manufactured bullshit you need to make a Mustang go into a skid at 138 miles an hour.

Yeah, I know. He had a Mustang. Ironic, right? At least I think that's the word. A 302 Mach 1, late '60s, with a back seat barely big enough for us to make what I was carrying. And yeah, that thing was fast.

But it was no mustang. Know what I mean?

It was no mustang.

Max circled back around in front of Adam and knelt into a crouch. "OK. So that's how the three of us got here. As for how you got—"

"Wait a minute. How did you guys actually get here, though? I was outside most of the afternoon and didn't see anybody pull up."

Sara touched his knee. "Far as I could tell, you were pretty lost in that horse when they got here."

"That's true, I guess. I couldn't believe that nighttime had already—"

Max lowered to his sit bones and wrapped his arms around his knees. "Look, you're running out of time. This is sort of a life-and-death thing." He paused. "Although that sounds a little dramatic when I say it out loud."

Adam craned his neck toward the door and back to Max, who held up his hand. "Don't worry, you're not going to die in this room at the hands of violent nature lovers. Greg, open that door so our friend here has one less thing to worry about."

Greg unlocked the dead bolt and walked over to the window. "Done. But we do need to get a decision from him."

"I know, I know. And to do that, he needs to know exactly what it is he's deciding." Max locked in on Adam. "So, did those stories you just heard shine any light on why we're here?"

"No, not really. Sounded like you were all talking about the same day and night, though. You kept saying 'that day' and 'that night.'"

Max shook his head. "Close, but no. Let's try another angle. Any thoughts about the last few days?"

"Well, now that I know this was all a setup, I'm not sure what to think."

"Let me rephrase. Notice anything different about the last few days?"

"I mean, I didn't have a phone. So that was different."

"And?"

"I didn't think as much about getting high."

"Why might that be?"

"I don't know. I guess I was distracted."

Max glanced over at Sara, who shrugged her shoulders. He looked back at Adam. "Distracted? We weren't going for distracted."

"What do you mean by 'going for'?"

"We were hoping that being seen by the ocean, being heard by the canyon, and being felt by that horse might show you a different way to live. Something you could share with other people, spread around, testify to. That was our assignment."

"If you're so worried about it, why don't you just do this testifying thing yourself? You seem to be pretty good at it. And who assigned—"

Greg didn't move from the window, just kept staring into nothing. "We're trying to help you, which will help us."

"Help you what? I don't—"

Max stood up and shoved his hands in his jeans pockets. "OK, you're out of time . . . almost a literal heartbeat away from two very different outcomes."

"But—"

"You can either keep breathing and follow a road similar to what we've shown you . . ." Max held his hand out to Sara and helped her up from the chair. "Or die in that puddle of piss you're lying in."

Adam looked down at the spotless floor between his feet, flecked only with mud from his boots. "What puddle of piss?"

"And just to prove nobody's out to hurt you"—Max whistled loud through his teeth, just like Adam used to do when he was calling his dog—"I thought you might want to see an old friend."

The scattering scrape of claws on wood sounded up the stairs, and through the open door bounded a huge black furball, weight lost to age restored, vibrancy drowned in disease returned, muzzle grayed by disease somehow a deep black again. Sooner bounced over to Adam and leaped into his lap, whimpering as he licked his face and pawed at his chest.

And not until then did Adam realize that none of this was what it seemed.

6

She blinked again against the drapes of wet atmosphere and immediately scampered back across the street, dodging the angled metal beasts as they coughed their foul particles into the air.

The pile of soft material that had smelled of potential was too enticing to resist, beckoning her to retrace her steps down the cavity. She paused at the puddle of piss that surrounded the scrap heap, her empty belly rumbling as she stretched across the foul pond in a careful search for an abandoned ration, maybe a speck of chicken nugget.

There was no sudden, spasmic jolt to her curiosity this time, no need to go scampering for safety. Only a warm tangle, reeking with the stench of hope, for the thin gray stray to leap into over the puddle, nudge, paw, and rearrange before turning three circles and curling up.

Where, finally, the little dog allowed a soft whimper to escape into the still-heaving folds of grimed cotton and polyester, their gently pulsing warmth offering a rhythmic, blunted relief from the glass and asphalt chaos of the street.

ABOUT THE AUTHOR

ALEX WOODARD lives with three horses, two dogs, two chickens, and two beautiful humans on a small ranch near the California coast.

His first novel found an early supporter in Woody Harrelson, who said "*Ordinary Soil* brings to haunting life the desperate realities of the American heartland, but also offers a glimpse into a better future . . . a call to action for all of us."

Analog Sun, a sequel to *Ordinary Soil*, is his second work of fiction. His nonfiction *For The Sender* book, album, and concert series has garnered praise from *Huffington Post* ("important, enlightening, and ultimately inspiring"), Deepak Chopra ("a beautiful tribute to the resilience of the human spirit"), Dr. Wayne Dyer ("an inspiring, thought-provoking, and life-changing work"), and *Billboard* magazine ("one of the year's most touching, unique releases"), among others. Alex has also toured nationally behind several critically acclaimed albums, earning a few prestigious industry nods while sharing the stage with some of his heroes.

Alex has stepped away from social media, but if you'd like to check out his work, you can find his stories and music at alexwoodard.com.